Harold Frederic

Mrs. Albert Grundy, The Mayfair Set

Observations in Philistia

Harold Frederic

Mrs. Albert Grundy, The Mayfair Set
Observations in Philistia

ISBN/EAN: 9783744745970

Printed in Europe, USA, Canada, Australia, Japan

Cover: Foto ©Andreas Hilbeck / pixelio.de

More available books at **www.hansebooks.com**

MRS·ALBERT·GRUNDY· OBSERVATIONS·IN·PHILISTIA

BY·HAROLD·FREDERIC

LONDON: JOHN·LANE·
NEW·YORK·
THE·MERRIAM·CO·
·MDCCCXCVI·

THE MAYFAIR SET

VI

MRS ALBERT GRUNDY

THE MAYFAIR SET

Foolscap 8vo.   3s. 6d. net each.

1. *The Autobiography of a Boy*, by G. S. STREET, *with Title-page designed by* C. W. FURSE.   [*5th Edition.*

2. *The Joneses and the Asterisks, a Story in Monologue*, by GERALD CAMPBELL, *with six Illustrations and a Title-page* by F. H. TOWNSEND.   [*2nd Edition.*

3. *Select Conversations with an Uncle (now extinct)*, by H. G. WELLS, *with a Title-page by* F. H. TOWNSEND.

4. *For Plain Women only*, by GEORGE FLEMING, *with Title-Page by* PATTEN WILSON.

5. *The Feasts of Autolycus, the Diary of a Greedy Woman, edited by* ELIZABETH ROBINS PENNELL, *with Title-Page by* PATTEN WILSON.

6. *Mrs Albert Grundy, Observations in Philistia*, by HAROLD FREDERIC, *with Title-Page by* PATTEN WILSON.

CONTENTS

CONTENTS

Presenting in Outline the Comfortable and Well-Regulated Paradox over which She Presides, and shewing its Mental Elevation

I SUPPOSE about the name there is no doubt. For sixty years we have followed that gifted gadabout and gossip, Heine, and called it Philistia. And yet, when one thinks of it, there may have been a mistake after all. Artemus Ward used to say that he had been able, with effort, to comprehend how it was possible to measure the distance between the stars, and even the dimensions and candle-power, so to speak, of those heavenly bodies; what beat him was how astronomers had ever found out their names. So I find myself wondering whether Philistia really is the right name for the land where She must be obeyed.

A

If so, it is only a little more the region of mysterious paradox and tricksy metamorphosis. We think of it always and from all time as given over to Her rule. We feel in our bones that there was a troglodyte Mrs Grundy; we imagine to ourselves a British matron contemporary with the cave bear and the woolly elephant. But her very antiquity only makes it more puzzling.

There is an old gentleman who always tries to prove to me that the French are really Germans, that the Germans are all Slavs, and that the Russians are strictly Tartars : that is to say, that in keeping count of the early races as they swarmed Westward we somehow skipped one, and have been wrong ever since. There must be some such explanation of how the domain which She sways came to be called Philistia.

I say this, because the old Philistia was tremendously masculine. It was the Jews who struck the feminine note. They used to swagger no end when they won a victory, and utilise it to the utmost limit of merciless savagery; but when it came their turn to be thrashed they filled the very heavens with complaining clamour. We got no hint that the Philistines ever failed to take their medicine like men.

Consider those splendid later Philistines, the Norsemen. In all their martial litera- ture there is no suggestion of a whine. They loved fighting for its own sake; next to braining their foes, they admired being themselves hewn into sections. They never blamed their gods when they had the worst of it. They never insisted that they were always right and their enemies invariably wrong. They cared nothing about all that. They demanded only fun. It was their victims, the Frankish and Irish monks, who shed women's tears and besought Providence to play favourites.

And here is the paradox. The children of these Berserker loins are become the minions of Mrs Grundy. By some magic she has enshrined Respectability in their temples. In one division of her empire she makes Mr Helmer drink tea; in

another she sets everybody reading the
Buchholz Family; in her chosen island
home her husband on the sunniest Sundays
carries an umbrella instead of a walking-
stick. Fancy the wild delirium of delight
with which the old Philistines would have
raided her homestead, chopping down her
Robert Elsmeres, impaling her Horsleys,
and making the skies lurid with the
flames of her semi-detached villa! Yet
we call her place Philistia !

I know the villa very well. It is quite
near to the South Kensington Museum.
The title "Fernbank" is painted on the
gate-posts. How well-ordered and comfortable does life beyond those posts remain !
Here are no headaches in the morning.
Here white-capped domestics move with
neat alertness along the avenues of gentle
routine, looking neither to the policeman
on the right nor fiery-jacketed Thomas
Atkins on the left. Here my friend Mr
Albert Grundy invariably comes home by
the Underground to dinner. Here his
three daughters—girls of a type with a

diminishing upper lip, with sharper chins and greater length of limb than of old—lead deeply washed existences, playing at tennis, smiling in flushed silence at visitors, feeding contentedly upon Mudie's stores, the while their mamma spreads the matrimonial net about the piano or makes tours of inspection among her outlying mantraps on the lawn. Here simpers the innocuous curate; here Uncle Dudley, who has seen life in Australia and the Far West, watches the bulbs and prunes the roses, and, I should think, yawns often to himself; here Lady Willoughby Wallaby's card diffuses refinement from the summit of the card-basket in the hall.

To this happy home there came but last week—or was it the week before—a parcel of books. There were four complete novels in twelve volumes—fruits of that thoughtful arrangement by which the fair reader in Philistia is given three distinct opportunities to decide whether she will read the story through or not. Mrs Albert is a busy woman, burdened with manifold responsibilities to Church and State, to organised charities, to popularised music, to art-work guilds and the Amalgamated Association of Clear Starchers, not to mention a weather-eye kept at all times upon all unmarried males : but she still finds time to open all these packets of new books herself. On this occasion she gave to her eldest, Ermyntrude, the first volume of a novel by Mrs ——. It doesn't matter what fell to the share of the younger Amy and Floribel. For herself she reserved the three volumes of the latest work of Mr ——.

She tells me now that words simply can *not* express her thankfulness for having done so. It seems the selection was not entirely accidental. She was attracted, she admits, by the charmingly dainty binding of the volumes, but she was also moved by an instinct, half maternal prescience, half literary recollection. She thought she remembered having seen the name of this man-writer before. Where ? It came to her like a flash, she says. Only a while ago he had a book called *A Bunch of Patrician Ladies* or something of that sort, which she almost made up her mind not to let the girls read at all, but at last, with some misgivings, permitted them to skim hastily, because though the morals were rocky—perhaps that wasn't her word —the society was very good. But this new book of his had not even that saving feature. Respectable people were only incidentally mentioned in it. Really it was quite *too* low. The chief figure was a farm-girl who for the most part skimmed milk or cut swedes in a field, and at other times behaved in a manner positively unmentionable. Mrs Albert told me she had locked the volumes up, after only partially perusing them. I might be sure *her* daughters never laid eyes on them. They had gone back to the library, with a note expressing surprise that such immoral books should be sent into any Christian family. What made the matter worse, she went on, was that Ermyntrude read in some paper, at a friend's house, that this man, whoever

he may be, was the greatest of English
novelists, and that this particular book of
his was a tragic work of the noblest and
loftiest order, which dignified the language.
She was sure she didn't know what
England was coming to, when reporters
were allowed to put things like that in
the papers.   Fortunately she only took in
The Daily Tarradiddle, which one could
always rely upon for sound views, and
which gave this unspeakable book precisely
the contemptuous little notice it deserved.

It was a relief, however—and here the
good matron visibly brightened up — to
think that really wholesome and improving
novels were still produced.   There was that
novel by Mrs——.   Had I read it ?   Oh,
I must lose no time !   Perhaps it was not
altogether so enchanting as that first im-
mortal work of hers, which had almost, one
might say, founded a new religion.   True,
one of the girls in it worked altar-cloths
for a church, and occasionally the other
characters broke out into religious conversation ; but there were no clergymen to

speak of, and the charm of the other's ecclesiastical mysticism was lacking. "To be frank, the first and last volumes were just a bit slow. But oh! the lovely second volume! A young Englishman and his sister go to Paris. They stumble right at the start into the most delightful, picturesque, artistic set. Think of it: Henri Regnault is personally introduced, and delivers himself of extended remarks——"

"I met an old friend of Regnault's at the Club the other day," I interposed, "who complained bitterly of that. He said it was insufferable impudence to bring him in at all, and still worse to make him talk such blather as is put into his mouth."

Mrs Albert sniffed at this Club friend and went on. That Paris part of the book seemed to her to just palpitate with life. It was Paris to the very letter— gay, intellectual, sparkling, and oh! *so* free! The young Englishman at once set up a romantic establishment in the heart of Fontainebleau Forest with a

French painter-girl. His sister was almost
as promptly debauched by an elderly French
sculptor. But you never lost sight of the
fact that the author was teaching a
valuable moral lesson by all this. Indeed,
that whole part of the book was called
"Storm and Stress." And all the while
you saw, too, how innately superior the
national character of the young Englishman was to that of the French people
about him. One *knew* that in good
time *he* would have a moral awakening,
and return to England, marry, settle
down, and make money in his business.
Side by side with this you saw the entire
hopelessness of any spiritual regeneration
in the French painter-girl or any of her
artistic set. And this was shown with
such delicate art—it was so *perfect* a
picture of the moral contrast between the
two nations—that the girls saw it at
once.

"Then the girls," I put in—"that is
to say, you didn't lock *this* book up?"

Mrs Albert lifted her eyebrows at me.

"How do you mean?" she asked. "Do you know who the author is? The idea! Why, the papers print whole columns about *anything* she writes. Every day you may see paragraphs about the mere prospect of books she hasn't even begun yet. I suppose such blatant publicity must be very distressing to her, but the public simply insist upon it. *The Daily Tarra-diddle* devoted an entire leader to this particular book. I assure you, all my friends are talking of nothing else—many of them people, too, whom you would not suspect of any literary tastes whatever, and who *never* read novels as a rule. But they don't regard *this* as a novel. They think of it—I quote Lady Willoughby Wallaby's exact words—as an exposition of those Christian principles which make our England what it is."

Setting forth the Untoward Circumstances under which the Right Tale was Unfolded in the Wrong Company

MUCH has been written about that variety of "cab-wit" which occurs to a man on his way home from dinner: the brilliant sallies he might have made, the smart retorts which would so bravely have reversed the balance of laughter had they only come in time. We are less frank about the other sort. No one dwells in type upon the manner in which we marshal our old jokes and arrange our epigrams as we drive along to the house of feasting.

No doubt the practice of getting up table-talk is going out. The three-bottle men took it to the grave with them, along with the snuff-box, and the toupee, and the feather-bed, and other amenities of the

Regency. There never was but one diner-out in the London of my knowledge who was at pains to prepare his conversations, each for its special occasion and audience, and he, poor man, broke down under the strain and disappeared from view. The others are too lazy, too indifferent, too cocksure of themselves, to go to all this bother. The old courtly sense of responsibility to the host is perished from among them. But none the less, the least dutiful and diligent of all their number does ask himself questions as the whirling rubber tyres bear him onward, and the cab-mirror shows him the face of a man to whom people ought to listen.

The question I asked myself, as I drove past the flaring shop windows of Old Brompton Road the other evening, was whether the Grundys would probably like my story of Nate Salsbury and the Citizen of South Bend, Indiana. A good deal depended upon the decision. It was a story which had greatly solidified my position in other hospitable quarters ; it could be

brought in *apropos* of almost anything,
or for that matter of quite nothing at
all ; it had never been printed, so far as
I know, in any of those American comic
papers which supply alike the dining-
rooms of Mayfair and the editorial offices
of Fleet Street with such humour as they
come into possession of ; and I enjoyed telling it. On the other hand, the Grundys
were old friends of mine, who would never
suspect that they had missed anything if
I preserved silence on the subject of South
Bend, and who would go on asking me
to dinner whether I told new tales or
not; moreover, their attitude towards fresh
jokes was always a precarious quantity,
and I had an uneasy feeling that if I told
my story to them and it failed to come
off, so to speak, I should never have the
same confidence in it again.

When I had entered the drawing-room
of Fernbank, shaken hands with Mrs
Albert Grundy and Ermyntrude, and stolen
a little glance about the circle as I walked
over to the fireplace, it had become clear

that the story was not to be told. Beside
the half-dozen of the family, including the
curate, there was a tall young man with
a very high collar, shoulders that sloped
down like a Rhine-wine bottle, and a
stern expression of countenance. Uncle
Dudley whispered to me, as we held our
hands over the asbestos, that he was a
literary party, and the son of old Sir
Watkyn Hump, who was a director in one
of Albert's companies. The other guests
were a stout and motherly lady in a cap
and a purplish smile, and a darkling young
woman with a black velvet riband around
her thin neck, and a look of wearied
indifference upon her face. This effect of
utter boredom did not visibly diminish
upon my being presented to Miss Wallaby.

I have an extremely well-turned little
brace of sentences with which to convey
the intelligence to a young lady that the
honour of taking her down to dinner has
fallen upon me—sentences which combine
professions of admiring pleasure with just
a grateful dash of respectful playfulness ;

they brought no new light into Miss
Wallaby's somewhat scornful *pince-nez.*
Decidedly I would not tell my South
Bend story *that* night !

But all the same I did. What led,up to
it I hardly know. It was at the ptarmigan
stage, I remember—or was it a capercail-
zie ?—and young Mr Hump had commented
upon the great joy of living in England,
where one could enjoy delicious game all
the year round, instead of in a country like
America, where the inhabitants notoriously
had nothing but fried salt pork to eat for
many months at a time. Perhaps it was
not worth while, but I ventured the cor-
recting remark that there was no season of
the year when one couldn't have eighteen
edible varieties of wild birds in America for
every one that England has ever heard of.
Mr Hump preened his chin about on the
summit of his collar and smiled with
superior incredulity. The others looked
grave. Mrs Grundy whispered to me
warningly, over her left shoulder, that Mr
Hump had made America his special sub-

ject, and wrote most vigorous and com-
minatory articles about it almost every
week. I was painfully conscious that Miss
Wallaby's cold right shoulder had been
still further withdrawn from me.

Well, it was at this grotesquely in-
auspicious moment that I told my story.
It is easy enough now to see that it was
sheer folly, madness if you like, to do so.
I was only too bitterly conscious of that
when I reviewed the events of the evening
in my homeward cab. It was *apropos* of
nothing under the wide sky. But at the
moment, I suppose, I hoped that it would
relieve the situation. In one sense it
did.

Baldly summarised, this is the tale.
Years ago the admirable Nate Salsbury
was on a " one-night-stand " tour with his
bright little company of comedians through
the least urban districts of Indiana, and
came upon South Bend, which is an important centre of the wagon-making in-
dustry, but is not precisely a focussing
point of dramatic traditions and culture.

In the vestibule of the small theatre that
evening there paced up and down a tall,
middle-aged, weasel-backed citizen, his
hands plunged deep in his pockets, doubt
and irresolution written all over his face.
As others paid their money and passed in
he would watch them with obvious longing ;
then he would go and study once more the
attractive coloured bill of the Company,
with its bevy of pretty girls in skirts just
short enough to disclose most enticing
little ankles ; then once more he would
resume his perplexed walk to and fro.   At
last he made up his mind, and approached
Salsbury with diffidence.   " Mister," he said,
" air you the boss of this show ? "   " What
can I do for you ? " asked Nate.   " Well—
no offence meant—but—can I—that is to
say—will it be all right to bring a lady to
your show ? "   " That, sir, depends ! " responded the manager firmly.   " Well," the
citizen went on, " what I was gittin' at is
this—can I be perfectly safe in bringin'
my wife here ? "   " Sir," said Salsbury with
dignity,   and   an   eye   trained   to   abstain

from twinkling, " it is no portion of my
business to inquire whether she is your
wife or not, but if she comes in here she's
got to behave herself ! "

A solitary note of laughter fell upon the
air when I had told this story, and on the
instant Uncle Dudley, perceiving that he
had made a mistake, dropped his napkin,
and came up from fishing for it on the
floor red-faced and dumb. All else was
deadly silence.

" I—I suppose they really weren't
married at all ? " said the curate, after a
chilling pause.

" Marriage, I regret to say, means next
to nothing in most parts of America,"
remarked Mr Hump, judicially. " The
most sacred ties are there habitually made
the subject of ribald jests. I have been
assured by a person who spent nearly three
weeks in the United States some years
since that it is an extremely rare experience
to meet an adult American who has not
been divorced at least once. This fact
made a vivid impression on my mind at

the time, and I—ahem!—have written frequently upon it since."

"I suppose the trouble arises from their all living in hotels—having no home life whatever," said Mrs Albert, with a kindly air of coming to my rescue.

"Who on earth told you that?" I began, but was cut short.

"I confess," broke in Miss Wallaby, with frosty distinctness of tone and enunciation, "that the assumption upon which the incident just related is based—the assumption that the la—woman referred to would probably misconduct herself in a place of public resort—seems to me startlingly characteristic of the country of which it is narrated. It has been truly said that the most valuable test of a country's actual, as distinct from its assumed, worth, is the respect it pays to its women. Both at Cheltenham and at Newnham the idea is steadily inculcated—I might say insisted upon as of paramount importance—that the nation's real civilisation rests upon the measure, not alone of chivalrous deference,

but of esteem and confidence which my sex,
by its devotion to duty, and its intellectual
sympathy with broad aims and lofty pur-
poses, is able to inspire and command."

"But I assure you," I protested feebly,
" the story I told was a joke."

"There are some subjects," interposed
Lady Willoughby Wallaby, the fixed smile
lighting up with an angry, winter-sunset
glow her inflamed countenance—" there are
some subjects on which it is best not to joke."

As she spoke she wagged a mitted thumb
at her hostess, and on the instant the ladies
rose.   Mr Hump hastened round to hold
the door open as they filed out, their heads
high in air, their skirts rustling indignantly
over the threshold.   Then he followed them,
closing the door with decision behind him.

" Gad, Albert," said Uncle Dudley, reach-
ing over for the port, " I don't wonder that
the pick of our young fellows go in for
marrying American girls."

"Pass it along !" remarked the father
of Mrs Albert's three daughters, in a voice
of confirmed dejection.

Annotating Sundry Points of Contact found to exist between the Lady and Contemporary Art

SCENE.—*Just inside the door of a studio.*
TIME.—*Last Sunday in March*, 5 *p.m.*

1st CITIZENESS. O, thank you *so* much !

2nd   do.   *So* good of you to come !

1st   do.   I *so* dote upon art !

2nd   do.   *So* kind of you to say so !

1st   do.   Thank you *so* much for asking us !

2nd   do.   Delighted, I'm sure ! Thank *you* for coming !

1st CITIZENESS. Not at all ! Thank you for—for thanking me for—Well—*good*-bye. (*Exit—with family group.*)

. . . .

HUSBAND OF 2nd CITIZENESS (*with gloom*). And who might *those* thankful bounders be ?

2nd CITIZENESS (*wearily*). O, don't ask *me* ! *I* don't know ! From Addison Road way, I should think.

. . . .

1st CITIZENESS (*outside*). Well ! If *that* thing gets into the Academy !

FAMILY GROUP. Did you notice the ridiculous way her hair was done ? Did you ever taste such tea in your life ? How yellow Mrs. General Wragg is getting to look in the daylight. Yes—there's our four-wheeler. (*Exeunt omnes.*)

22

THE above is not intended for presentation upon any stage—not even that of the Independent Theatre. It has been cast into the dramatic mould merely for convenience' sake. It embodies what I chiefly remember about Picture Sunday.

It has come to be my annual duty—a peculiarly hardy, not to say temerarious, annual—to convoy Mrs Albert Grundy and her party about sections of Chelsea and Brompton on the earlier of the two Show Sabbaths. I drifted into this function through having once shared an attic with a young painter, whose colleagues used to come to borrow florins of him whenever one of his pictures disappeared from any shop window, and so incidentally formed my acquaintance. My claim nowadays upon their recollection is really very slight. I just know them well enough to manage the last Sunday in March: even that might be awkward if they were not such good-natured fellows.

But it would be difficult to persuade Mrs Albert of this. That good lady is

wont, when the playfully benignant mood
is upon her, to describe me as her con-
necting link with Bohemia. She probably
would be puzzled to explain her meaning ;
I certainly should. But if she were pro-
vided with affidavits setting forth the
whole truth—viz., that my entire income
is derived from an inherited part-interest
in an artificial-ice machine ; that there are
two clergymen on the committee of my
only club ; that I am free from debt ; and
that I play duets on the piano with my
sister—still would she cling to the belief
that I am a young man with an extremely
gay, rakish side, who could make thrilling
revelations of Bohemia if I would. Of
course, I am never questioned on the
subject ; but I can see that it is a point
upon which the faith of Fernbank is firmly
grounded. Often Mrs Albert's conversation cuts figure-eights on very thin ice
when we are alone, as if just to show me
that *she* knows. More than once I have
discovered Ermyntrude looking furtively at
me, as the wistful shepherd-boy on the

plains of Dura might have gazed at the distant haze overhanging bold, unspeakable Babylon. I rarely visit the house but Uncle Dudley winks at me. However, nothing is ever asked me about the dreadful things with which they suppose me to be upon intimate terms.

It seemed for a long time, on Sunday, as if an easy escape had been arranged for me by Providence. At two o'clock, the hour appointed for our crusade, a heavy fog overhung everything. Looking out from the drawing-room windows, only the very nearest of the neatly trimmed firs on the lawn were to be distinguished. The street beyond was utter blackness.

At three o'clock the ladies took off their bonnets. It was really too bad. Uncle Dudley, strolling in from his nap in the library, suggested that with a lantern we might visit some of the nearer studios: "not necessarily for publication, but as a guarantee of good faith." Mrs Albert turned a look of tearful vexation upon him, before which he fled.

"There's this consolation," she remarked presently, holding me with an unwavering eye : " if we are to be defrauded out of our expedition to-day, that will furnish all the more reason why you should take us next Sunday—*the* Sunday.   You have often talked of having us see the Academicians at home—but we've never been."

" I remember that there has been talk about it," I said ; " but hardly that the talk was mine.   Truth is, I don't know a single Academician, even by sight."

It was clear that they did not believe me.   Mrs Albert continued : " Lady Wallaby expressed surprise, only last evening, that we should consent to go about among the outsiders.   She and her daughter *never* do."

"Outsiders !" I was tempted into saying. " Why, they can paint the head off the Academy ! "

Miss Timby-Hucks simpered outright. "You do say such droll things !" she remarked, somewhat obscurely.   " Mamma always declares that you remind her of the *Sydney Bulletin*."

" Whom *do* you take to the Academy
Show Sunday ?—or perhaps I oughtn't to
ask," came from Ermyntrude.

" No, we have no right to inquire," said
Mrs Albert ; and I turned to the window
and the enshrouded lawn once more.

All at once the fog lifted. The bonnets
were produced again. Nearly three hours
of daylight remained to us. Tidings that
the horse was too lame to be taken out only
staggered Mrs Albert for the briefest fraction
of time. There were still four-wheelers in
Gilead. Besides, if the driver happened to
be sober, he would know the streets so
much better than their stupid coachman.
This would be of advantage, because time
was so limited. We should have to just
run in, say "How-d'ye-do," take a flying
look round, and scamper out again, Mrs
Albert said. By firmly adhering to this
rule, she estimated that we might do sixteen
or seventeen studios.

Heaven alone knows how many we did
" do." Nor have I any clear recollections
of what we saw. A confused vision remains

to me of long hall-ways lined with frames
and packing-cases; half-an-acre, more or
less, of painted canvas, out of which only
here and there a pair of bright eyes, a glow-
ing field of poppies, or the sheen from a
satin gown, fixed itself disconnectedly on
the memory; hordes and hordes of tall
young women helping themselves to tea and
cakes; and always the pathetic figure of
the artist's wife, or sister, tired to very
death, standing by the door with a wearied
smile on her lips, and the polite falsehood,
"So good of you to come!" on her tongue.
I wondered, I remember, if she never forgot
herself and said instead, "So kind of you
to go!" But under Mrs Albert's system
there was no time to wait and see.

Once, indeed, we dallied over our task.
Mrs Albert encountered a lady from Worm-
wood Scrubs of her acquaintance, who was
indiscreet enough to mention that she had
been asked to stop here for supper. The
news spread through the petticoated portion
of my group as by magic. Miss Timby-
Hucks came over and asked me, so audibly

that the artist-host had to blush and turn away, if I didn't think it would be a deliciously romantic experience to sup in one of these lofty studios, with the gaslight on the armour, and the great, solemnly silent pictures looking down upon us as we ate. Mrs Albert lingered for some time looking at this artist's work with her head on one side, and eyes filled with rapt, dreamy enjoyment—but nothing came of it.

It was after we had been back in Fernbank for an hour or more—our own cold repast nearly over — that Mrs Albert thought of something. She laid down her fork with a gesture of annoyance. "It has just occurred to me," she said; "we never went to that Mr Whistler's, whose pictures are on exhibition in Bond Street. Everybody's talking about him, and I did so want not to miss his studio."

"I don't think he has a Show Sunday," I said. "I never heard of it, if he has."

"O no, it is only these last few weeks that anybody has heard of him,"

Mrs Albert replied. " I read the first announcement about his beautiful pictures in *The Daily Tarradiddle* only the other day."

"Whistler ? Whistler ? " put in Uncle Dudley. "Why, surely *he's* not new. Why—I remember—he was mixed up in a law-suit, wasn't it, years ago ? "

" O no, Dudley," responded Mrs Albert ; " I was under that same impression, till Lady Wallaby set me right. It seems that was another man altogether—some foreign adventurer who pretended to be able to paint and imposed upon people —don't you recall how *The Tarradiddle* exposed him ?—and Mr Burnt-Jones had him arrested, or something—O, quite a dreadful person. But *this* Mr Whistler is an Englishman. I read in *The Illustrated London News* that he represented modern British Art. That alone would make it quite clear it was a different man. I did so want to see him ! Lady Wallaby tells me she has heard he is extremely amusing in his conversation —and quite presentable manners, too."

"Why don't you ask him to dinner?" said Mr Albert Grundy. "If he's amusing it's more than most of the men you drum up are."

"You seem to think *everybody* can be asked to dinner, Albert," the lady of the house replied. "Artists don't dine —unless they are in the Academy, of course. Tea, yes—or perhaps supper; but one doesn't ask people to meet them at dinner. It's like actors—and—and non-commissioned officers."

Affording a Novel and Subdued Scientific Light, by which divers Venerable Problems may be Observed Afresh

" IT is my opinion," said Uncle Dudley, stretching out his slippered feet, and thrusting his thumbs into the armholes of his waistcoat—" it is my opinion that women are different from men."

" Several commentators have advanced this view," I replied. " For example, it has been noted that the gentle sex cross a muddy street on their heels, whereas we skip over on our toes."

" That is interesting if true," responded Uncle Dudley. " What I mean is that all this talk about the human race is humbug. There are *two* human races ! And they are getting wider apart every few minutes, too ! "

"Have you mentioned this to any one?" I asked.

Uncle Dudley went on developing his theme. "I daresay that for millions of years after the re-separation of the sexes this difference was too slight to be noticed at all. The cave man, for instance—the fellow who went around hunting the Ichthyosaurus with a brick tied on the end of an elm club, and spent the whole winter underground sucking the old bones, and then whittling them up into Runic buttons for the South Kensington Museum: I suppose, now, that his wife and sister-in-law, say, didn't strike him as being specially different from himself—except, of course, in that they only got plain bones and gristle and so on to eat, whereas all the marrow and general smooth-sailing in meats went his way. *You* can't imagine *him* saying to himself: 'These female people here are not of my race at all. They are of another species. They are in reality as much my natural enemies as that long-toed, red-headed,

c

brachycephalous tramp living in the gum-
tree down by the swamp, who makes
offensive gestures as I ride past on my
tame *Ursus spelœus*'—now, can you?"

I frankly shook my head. "No, I
don't seem to be able to imagine that.
It would be almost as hard as to guess
off-hand where, when, and how you caught
this remarkable scientific spasm."

Uncle Dudley smiled. He rose, and
walked with leisurely lightness up and
down in front of the chimney-piece, still
with his palms spread like little mis-
placed wings before his armpits. He
smiled again. Then he stopped on the
hearth-rug and looked down amiably
upon me.

"Well—what d'ye think? There's
something in it, eh?"

"My dear fellow," I began, "what
puzzles me is——"

"O, I don't mean to say that I've
worked it all out," put in Uncle Dudley,
reassuringly. "Why, I get puzzled myself, every once in a while. But I'm on

the right track, my boy; and, as they say in Adelaide, I'm going to hang to it like a pup to a root."

"How long have you been this way?" I asked, with an affectation of sympathy.

Uncle Dudley answered with shining eyes. "Why, if you'll believe me, it seems now as if I'd had the germs of the idea in my mind ever since I came back to England, and began living here at Fernbank. But the thing dawned upon me—that is to say, took shape in my head—less than a fortnight ago. It all came about through being up here one evening with nothing to read, and my toe worse than usual, and Mrs Albert having been out of sorts all through dinner. Somehow, I felt all at once that I'd got to read scientific works. I couldn't resist it. I was like Joan of Arc when the cows and sheep took partners for a quadrille. I heard voices— Darwin's and—and—Benjamin Franklin's —and—lots of others. I hobbled down-stairs to the library, and I brought up

a whole armful of the books that Mrs
Albert bought when she expected Lady
Wallaby was going to be able to get her
an invitation to attend the Hon. Mrs
Coon-Alwyn's Biological Conversaziones.
Look there! What do you say to that
for ten days' work? And had to cut
every leaf, into the bargain!"

I gazed with respect at the considerable
row of books he indicated: books for the
most part bound in the scarlet of the In-
ternational Series or the maroon of Contemporary Science, but containing also
brown covers, and even green "sport"
varieties.

"Well, and what is it all about?" I
asked. "Why have you read these things?
Why not the reports of the Commission
on Agricultural Depression, or Lewis
Morris's poems, or even——" but my
imagination faltered and broke.

"It was instinct, my boy," returned
Uncle Dudley, with impressive confidence.
"There had been a thought—a great idea
—growing and swelling in my head ever

since I had been living in this house.
But I couldn't tell what it was. As you
might say, it was wrapped up in a cocoon,
like the larvæ of the lepidoptera—ahem !
—and something was needed to bring it
out."

"When I was here last you were trying
Hollands with quinine bitters," I remarked
casually.

"Don't fool!" Uncle Dudley admonished
me. "I'm dead in earnest. As I said,
it was pure instinct that led me to these
books. They have made everything clear.
I only wanted their help to get the husk
off my discovery, and hoist it on my back,
as it were, and bring it out here in the
daylight. And so now you know what
I'm getting at when I say: Women are
different from Men."

"That is the discovery, then?" I
inquired.

Uncle Dudley nodded several times.
Then he went on, with emphasised slowness: "I have lived here now for four
years, seeing my sister-in-law every day,

watching Ermyntrude grow up to woman-
hood and the little girls peg along behind
her, and meeting the female friends who
come here to see them—and, sir, I tell
you, they're not alone a different sex :
they're a different animal altogether !
Take my word for it, they're a species by
themselves."

" Miss Timby-Hucks is certainly very
much by herself," I remarked.

My friend smiled. " And not altogether
her own fault either," he commented.
" But, speaking of science, it's remarkable
how, when you once get a firm grip on
a big, central, main-guy fact, all the little
facts come in of their own accord to sup-
port it. Now, there's that young simpleton
you met here at dinner a while ago: I
mean Eustace Hump. Do you know that
both Ermyntrude and the Timby-Hucks,
and even Miss Wallaby, think that that
chap is a perfect ideal of masculine wit
and beauty ? You and I would hesitate
about using him to wad a horse-pistol
with : but there isn't one of those girls

that wouldn't leap with joy if he began
proposing to her ; and as for their mothers,
why, the old ladies watch him as a king-
fisher eyes a tadpole."

"Your similes are exciting," I said ;
"but what do they go to show ? "

"My dear fellow, science can show anything.   I haven't gone all through it yet,
but I tell you, it's wonderful !   Take this,
for instance "—he reached for a green
book on the mantel, and turned over the
leaves—"now listen to this.   The book
is written by a man named Wallace—
nice, shrewd - looking old party by his
picture, you can see—and this is what
he says on page 285 : 'Some peahens
preferred an old pied peacock ; a Canada
goose paired with a Bernicle gander ; a
male widgeon was preferred by a pintail
duck to its own species ; a hen canary
preferred a male greenfinch to either linnet,
goldfinch, siskin, or chaffinch.'   Now, do
you see that ?   The moment my eyes first
lighted on that, I said to myself: 'Now
I understand about the girls and Eustace
Hump.'   Isn't it clear to you ? "

" Absolutely," I assented. " You ought
to read a paper at the Royal Aquarium
—before the Balloon Society, I mean."

" And then look at this," Uncle Dudley
went on, with animation. " Now, you
and I would ask ourselves what on earth
such a gawky, spindling, poor - witted
youngster as that thought he was doing
among women, anyhow. But you turn
over the page, and here you have it :
' Goat - suckers, geese, carrion vultures,
and many other birds of plain plumage
have been observed to dance, spread their
wings or tails, and perform strange love-
antics.' Doesn't that fasten Hump to the
wall like a beetle on a pin, eh ? "

" But I am not sure that I entirely
follow its application to your original
point," I suggested.

" About women, you mean ? My boy,
in science everything applies. The woods
are full of applications. But seriously,
women *are* different. As I said, in the
barbarism at the back of beyond this
divergence started. With the beginning

of what we call civilisation, it became
more and more marked. The progress
of the separation increases nowadays by
square-root—or whatever you call it. The
sexes are wider apart to-day than ever.
They like each other less; they quarrel
more. You can see that in the Divorce
Courts, in the diminished proportion of
early marriages, in the increasing evidences
of domestic infelicity all about one."

I could not refrain from expressing the
fear that all this boded ill for the per-
petuity of the human race.

Uncle Dudley is a light-hearted man.
He was not depressed by the apprehensions
to which I had given utterance. Instead
he hummed pleasantly to himself as he
put Wallace back on the shelf. He began
chuckling as a moment later he bethought
himself to fill our glasses afresh.

"Did I ever tell you my cat story?"
he asked cheerily, testing the knob to see
that the door was shut. "Once a little
boy came in to his father and said : 'Pa,
we won't be troubled any more with those

cats howling about on our roof at night. I've just been looking out of the upstairs window, and they're all out there fighting and screaming and tearing each other to pieces. There won't be one of them alive by morning ! ' Then the father replied : ' My son, you imagine a vain thing. When increasing years shall have furnished your mind with a more copious store of knowledge, you will grasp the fact that all this commotion and dire disturbance which you report to me only signifies more cats.' "

At this juncture the servant came in with the soda-water. We talked no more of science that evening.

*Touching the Experimental Graft of a
Utilitarian Spirit upon the Aesthetic
Instinct in our Sisters*

I HAD strolled about the galleries of Bur-
lington House for a couple of hours on
Press Day, looking a little at pictures here
and there, but for the most part contem-
plating with admiration the zeal and good
faith of the ladies and gentlemen who
stopped, note-book in hand, before every
frame : when some one behind me gave
a friendly tug at my sleeve. I turned,
to find myself confronted by a person I
seemed not to know—a small young woman
in an alpine hat and a veil which masked
everything about her face except its denti-
gerous smile. Even as I looked I was
conscious of regret that, if acquaintances
were to be made for me in this spontaneous

fashion, destiny had not selected instead
a certain tall, slender, dark young lady,
clad all in black and cock's-plumes, whom
I had been watching at her work of note-
taking in room after room, with growing
interest.   Then, peering   more   closely
through the veil, I discovered that I was
being accosted by Miss Timby-Hucks.

"You didn't know me!" she said, with
a vivacious half-giggle, as we shook hands ;
"and you're not specially pleased to see
me ; and you're asking yourself, 'What
on earth is she doing here?'   Now, don't
deny it!"   ·

"Well, you know," I made awkward
response—"of course—*Press* day——"

"Ah, but I belong to the Press," said
Miss Timby-Hucks.

"Happy Press!   And since when?"

"O it's nearly a fortnight now.   And
most *interesting* I find the work.   You
know, for a long time now I've been *so*
restless, *so* anxious to find some opening
to a real career, where I might be my
genuine self, and be an active part of the

great whirling stream of existence, and
concentrate my mind upon the actualities
of life—don't you yourself think it will
be *just* the thing for me ? "

"Undoubtedly," I replied without hesitation.   "And do you find focussing
yourself on the actualities—ah—remun-
erative ? "

"Well," Miss Timby-Hucks explained,
"nothing of mine has been printed yet,
you see, so that I don't know as to that.
But I am assured it will be all right.   You
see, I'm *very* intimate with a cousin of Mrs
Umpelbaum, who is the wife of the proprietor of *Maida Vale*, and in that way
it came about.   Lady-reporters never have
any chance, I am told, unless they have
friends in the proprietor's family, or know
the editor extremely well.   It all goes by
favour, like—like———"

"Like the dearest of all the actualities,"
I put in.   "But how is it they don't print
your stuff ? "

"I haven't written any, as yet.   The
difficulty was to find a subject," Miss

Timby-Hucks rejoined. "O that awful 'subject'! I thought and thought and thought till my head was fit to burst. I went to see Mrs Umpelbaum herself, and asked her to suggest something. You know she writes a great deal for the paper herself. She said they hadn't had any 'Reminiscences of Carlyle' now for some weeks; but afterwards she agreed with me that would not be quite the thing for one to *begin* with. She couldn't suggest anything else, except that I should have a chat with my dressmaker. Very often in that way, she said, lady-reporters get the most *entertaining* revelations of gossip in high life. But it happened that just then it was not—not exactly convenient—for me to call upon my dressmaker; and so *that* suggestion came to nothing, too."

"I had no idea lady-journalism was so difficult," I remarked, with sympathy.

"O indeed, yes!" Miss Timby-Hucks went on. "One can't expect to be *en rapport*, as we journalists say, with Society, without spending a great deal of money.

There is one lady-reporter, Mrs Umpelbaum told me, who has made quite a leading position for herself, solely through hair-dressers and American dentists. But I don't mind admitting that that would involve more of an outlay than I could afford, just at the moment."

"So you never got a subject ?" I asked.

"Yes ; finally I did. I was over at the Grundys', telling my troubles, and Uncle Dudley—you know, being so much with the girls, I always call him that—Uncle Dudley said that the fashionable thing now was interviews, and that lady-journalists did this better than gentlemen-reporters because they had more nerve. By that I suppose he meant a more delicate nervous organisation, quicker to grasp and absorb fine shades of character. But that hardly helped me, because whom was I to interview, and about what ? *That* was the question ! But Uncle Dudley thought a moment, and was ready with a suggestion. Everything depended, he said, upon making a right start. I must pick out a personality and a theme

at once non-contentious and invested with
popular interest.   His idea was that I should
begin by interviewing Mr T. M. Healy on
' The Decline of the Deep-Sea Mock-Turtle
Fisheries on the West Coast of Ireland.'   If
I could get Mr Healy to talk frankly on
this subject, he felt sure that I should
chain public attention at a bound."

" Superb !" I cried.   " And did you do
it ? "

" No," Miss Timby-Hucks confessed ;   " I
went to the House and sent in my card,
but it was another Irish Member who came
out to see me—I think his name was Mul-
hooly.   He was very polite, and explained
that since some recent sad event in one of
the Committee Rooms, fifteen I think its
number was, it was the rule of his party
that, when a lady sent in a card to one
Member, some other Member answered it.
It prevented confusion, he said, and was
not in antagonism to the expressed views
of the Church."

" Talking of nothing," I said, leading the
way over to a divan, on which we seated

ourselves: "you seem to have finally
secured a subject. I assume you are doing
the Academy for *Maida Vale*."

"Yes," replied Miss Timby-Hucks with
gentle firmness; "you might say I have
done it. I have been here since the very
minute the doors opened, and I've gone
twelve times round. I wish I could have
seen you earlier. I should *so* like to have
had your opinion of the various works as
we passed."

"It is better not," I commented.
"There are ladies present."

The lady-reporter looked at me for a
furtive instant dubiously. Then she smiled
a little under her veil. "You *do* say such
odd things!" she remarked. "I am glad to
see that a great many ladies *are* present.
It shows how we are securing our proper
recognition in journalism. I believe there
are actually more of us here than there are
gentlemen-reporters—I should say gentle-
men-critics. And it is the same in art, too.
You can see—I've counted them up in my
catalogue here—there are this year two

D

hundred and forty-four lady-artists exhibiting in this Academy three hundred and forty-six works of art. Think of that! Fifty of them are described as Mrs, and there are one hundred and ninety-four who are unmarried."

" Think of *that !* " I retorted.

" And there are among them," Miss Timby-Hucks went on, " one Marchioness, one Countess, one Baroness, and one plain Lady. I am going to begin my article with this. I think it will be interesting, don't you ? "

" I'd be careful not to particularise about the plain Lady," I suggested. " That might be *too* interesting."

She was over-full of her subject to smile. " No, I mean," she said, " as showing how the ranks of British Art are being filled from the very highest classes, and are appealing more and more to the female intellect. I don't believe it will occur to any one else to count up in the catalogue. So that will be original with me—to enlighten my sex as to the glorious part they play in this year's Academy."

"But have you seen their pictures?" I asked, repressing an involuntary groan.

"Every one!" replied Miss Timby-Hucks. "They are all good. There isn't what I should call a bad one—that is, a Frenchy or immoral one—among them. I shall say that, too, in my criticism; but of course I shall have to word it carefully, because I fancy Mr Umpelbaum is a foreigner of some sort—and you know they're all so sensitive about the superiority of British Art."

"It is their nature; they can't help it," I pointed out. "They try their best, however, to master these unworthy emotions. Sometimes, indeed, their dissimulation reaches a really high plane of endeavour."

"They have nothing at all on the Continent like our Royal Academy, I am told," said Miss Timby-Hucks. "That isn't generally known, is it? I had thought of saying it."

"It will be a safe statement," I assured her. "You might go further, and assert that no other country at any stage of its

history has had anything like the Royal
Academy.   It is the unique blossom of
British civilisation."

Miss Timby-Hucks seemed to like the
phrase, and made a note of it on the back
of her catalogue. "Yes," she continued,
"I thought of making my criticism general,
dealing with things like that. But I've
got some awfully interesting figures to put
in.   For example, there are sixty-eight
Academicians and Associates exhibiting :
they have one hundred and thirty-five oil
paintings, sixteen water-colour or black-
and-white drawings, eight architectural
designs, and twenty-three pieces of sculp-
ture—a total of one hundred and eighty-
two works of art, or two and sixty-seven
hundredths each.   I got at that by dividing
the total number of works by the total
number of Academicians.   Do you think
any one else will be likely to print that
first in a daily paper ?   Mrs Umpelbaum
told me that *Maida Vale* made a special
point of new facts.   I don't think I shall
say much about the pictures themselves.

What *is* there to say about pictures by the
Academicians ?   As I told mamma this
morning, they wouldn't be Academicians if
they didn't paint good pictures, would
they ? and good pictures speak for themselves.   Of course, I shall describe the
subjects of Sir Frederic's pictures—by
the way, what *is* a Hesperides ?—and
some of the others : I'll get you to pick
out for me a few leading names.   But I
shall make my main point the splendid
advance of lady-artists—I heard some one
say in the other room there'd never been
half so many before—and the elevating
effect this has upon British Art.   In fact,
mightn't I say that is what makes British
Art what it is to-day ? "

"It is one of the reasons, undoubtedly,"
I assented, as I rose.   "There are others,
however."

"Yes, I know," said Miss Timby-Hucks :
" the diffusion of Christian principles
amongst us, our high national morality,
and the sanctity of the English home.
Mrs Albert said only last night that these

lay at the very foundation of British art."

" Mrs Albert is a woman of discernment," I said, making a gesture of farewell.

But Miss Timby-Hucks on the instant thought of something. Her eyes glistened, her two upper front teeth gleamed. " O, it's just occurred to me ! " she exclaimed, moving nearer to my side, and speaking in confidential excitement. " I know now how that lady-reporter manages with the hairdressers and dentists. She doesn't pay them money at all. She mentions their names in the papers instead. How dull of me not to have thought of that before ! Why—yes—I will !—I'll put my dressmaker among the Private View celebrities ! "

One likes to be civil to people who are obviously going to succeed in the world. I forthwith took Miss Timby-Hucks out to luncheon.

Relating to Various Phenomena attending the Progress of the Sex along Lines of the Greatest Resistance

"My own idea," said Uncle Dudley, "is that women ought to be confined to barracks during elections just the same as soldiers."

"I was quite prepared to find *you* entertaining views of that character," remarked Miss Wallaby, with virginal severity. "Men who have wandered about the less advanced parts of the earth, and spent long periods of time in contact with inferior civilisations, quite generally do feel that way. Life in the Colonies, and in similar rude and remote regions, does produce that effect upon the masculine mind. But here in England, the nerve-centre of the English-speaking race, the point of concentration from which radiate all the impulses of

55

refinement and culture that distinguish our
generation, men are coming to see these
matters in a different light. They no
longer refuse to listen to the overwhelming
arguments in favour of entire feminine
equality——"

"Oh, *I* admit *that* at once," broke in
Uncle Dudley. "But do women nowadays
believe in equality among themselves? In
my youth they used to devote pretty well
all their energies to showing how much
superior they were to other women."

"I spoke of the masculine attitude," said
Miss Wallaby, coldly. "Viewed intelli-
gently, the gradations and classifications
which we maintain among ourselves, at the
cost of such infinite trouble and personal
self-sacrifice, are the very foundation upon
which rests the superstructure of British
Society."

"I admit that, too," Uncle Dudley
hastened to put in. "Really, we are getting on very nicely."

Miss Wallaby ignored the interruption
altogether. "The point is," she went on,

" that the male mind in England is coming
—with characteristic slowness, no doubt,
but still coming—to recognise the necessity
of securing the very fullest and most complete participation of my sex in public
affairs.   As the diffusion of enlightenment
progresses, men will more and more abandon
the coarse and egoistic standards of their
days.of domination by brute force, and turn
instead to the ideals of purity and sweetness
which Woman in Politics typifies.   It has
been observed that one may pick out the
future rulers of England in each coming
generation by scanning the honour-lists of
Oxford and Cambridge.   How happy a
day it will be for England, and civilisation,
when this is said of Girton and Newnham
as well ! "

"I spent a summer in the State of Maine
once, some years ago," said Uncle Dudley.
"That's the State, you know, where they've
had a Prohibition law now for nearly forty
years.   The excess of females over males
is larger there, I believe, than it is any-
where else in the world—owing to the fact

that all the young men who are worth their salt emigrate to some other State as soon as they've saved up enough for a railway-ticket. The men that you do see lounging around there, in the small villages, are all minding the baby, or sitting on the door-step shelling peas, or out in the backyard, with their mouths full of clothes-pins, hanging up sheets and pillow-cases on the line to dry. The women there take a very active part in politics—and every census shows that Maine's population has diminished. Shipbuilding has almost ceased, farms are being abandoned yearly, the State is mortgaged up to its eyebrows, and you get nothing but fried clams and huckle-berry-pie for breakfast—but, of course, I suppose there *is* a good deal of purity and sweetness."

Miss Wallaby rose and walked away from us; the black velvet riband around her neck, the glint of gas-light on her eye-glasses, the wearied haughtiness on her swarthy, high-nosed face, seemed to unite in saying to us that we were very poor creatures indeed.

"She's been down to the Retired
Licensed Victuallers' Division of Surrey,
you know," exclaimed Uncle Dudley,
"making speeches in favour of the sitting
Member, old Sir Watkyn Hump."

"Ah, that accounts for the milk in the
cocoa-nut," I remarked.

"Well, no," my friend mused aloud,
"I fancy *young* Hump accounts for that.
See—she's gone and cut him out from
under the Timby-Hucks's guns."

It was at one of Mrs Albert Grundy's
evenings at home, and Uncle Dudley and
I now had possession of a quiet corner
to ourselves. From this pleasant vantage-
ground we indolently surveyed the throng
surrounding Mrs Albert at the piano end
of the room, and stretching off through
the open double doors into the adjoining
chamber—a throng of dazzling arms and
shoulders, of light-hued satins and fluffy
stuffs, of waving feathers, and splendid
piles of braided hair, and mostly comely
faces wreathed in politic smiles. Here
and there the mass of pinks and whites

and creams was broken abruptly by a
black coat with a hat under its sleeve.
Dudley and I idly commented upon the
fact that almost all these coats belonged
to undersized elderly men, generally with
spectacles and a grey beard, and we noted
with placid interest that as they came in
—announced in stentorian tones as Mr
and Mrs So-and-so—their wives as a
rule were several inches taller and many
many years younger than themselves.

Then it was entertaining, too, to watch
Mrs Albert shake hands with these new-
comers.   She knew just at what angle
each preferred that ceremony, keeping
her knuckles well down in welcoming
the more sophisticated and up-to-date
people from about Cromwell Road and
the Park, but elevating them breast-high
to greet those from around Brompton
way, and hoisting them quite up to the
chin-level with the guests from beyond
Earl's Court, who were still in the toils of
last year's fashions.

"Smart woman, that sister of mine!"

said Uncle Dudley. " See the way she's manœuvred her shoulder around in front of the Timby-Hucks's nose, so as to head her off from getting in and being introduced to the Hon. Mrs Coon-Alwyn. And —hello ! by George, she's won !—there's the Dowager Countess of Thames-Ditton coming in ! You'll never know the anguish, my boy, that was caused by the uncertainty whether she would come or not. Emily hasn't been able to eat these past four days, expecting every moment the knock of the postman bringing her ladyship's refusal to come. The only thing that enabled her to keep up, she said, was fixing her mind resolutely on the fact that the aristocracy are notoriously impolite about answering invitations. But now, happy woman—her cup is fairly running over. This is a great night for Fernbank. And—look !—hanged if that girl isn't trying to edge her way in there, too ! See how prettily Emily managed that ? Oh, Timby-Hucks ! Timby-Hucks ! you've put your foot in it this time.

You'll never figure on the free-list for
this show again."

Misfortune indeed claimed Miss Timby-
Hucks for its very own. Mrs Albert had
twice adroitly interposed her well-rounded
shoulders between that enterprising young
woman and social eminence—the second
time with quite obvious determination of
purpose. And there, too, behind the door,
young Mr Hump bent his sloping shoulders
and cliff-like collar humbly over Miss
Wallaby's chair, listening with all his
considerable ears to her selected monologues. Ah, the vanity of human aspira-
tions !

Casting an heroic glance over the field
of defeat, Miss Timby-Hucks's eye lighted
upon our corner, and on the instant her
two upper front teeth gleamed in a smile
of relief. At all events, *we* were left—
and she came towards us with a decisive
step.

" I've hardly seen you since the
Academy," she said in her sprightly way
to me, after we had all shaken hands, and

she had seated herself between us on the
sofa.

"And how did your article come out?"
I asked politely.

"Oh, it never came out at all," she
replied. "It seems it got left over too
long. The editor *said* it was owing to the
pressure of interesting monkey-language
matter upon his columns; but *I* believe
it was just because I'm a lady journalist,
and so does the cousin of Mrs Umpelbaum,
the proprietor's wife. It must have been
that—because, long after the editor gave
this excuse, there were the daily papers
still printing their criticisms, 'Eleventh
Notice of the Royal Academy,' 'The
Spring Exhibitions—Fourteenth Article,'
and so on. I taxed him with it—told
him I heard they had some still left, that
they were going to begin printing again
after the elections were over—but he said
it was different with dailies. All *they*
needed were advertisements and market
reports, and police news, and telegrams
about the Macedonian frontier, and they

could print art criticisms and book reviews
whole years after they should have appeared, because nobody ever read them
when they were printed—but weeklies had
to be absolutely up to date."

"Evil luck does pursue you!" I said,
compassionately. "So you haven't got
into print at all?"

"O I'm not a bit cast down," replied
Miss Timby-Hucks, with jaunty confidence.
"There's no such word as fail in *my*
book. The way to succeed is just to keep
pegging away. I know of one lady-
journalist who went every day for nine
weeks to interview the Countess of Wimps
about her second son's having been warned
off Newmarket Heath. Every day she was
refused admittance—once she got into the
hall and was put out by a brutal footman
—but it never unnerved her. Each
morning she went again. And she
would have succeeded by this time,
probably — only the Countess suddenly
left England to spend the summer in
Egypt."

"Yes, Wady Halfa *has* its advantages, even in July," said Uncle Dudley. "It is warm, and there are insects, but one is allowed by law to kill them—in Egypt."

Illustrating the operation of Vegetables and Feminine Duplicity upon the Concepts of Maternal Responsibility

I FELT that I was on sufficiently intimate terms with Mrs Albert Grundy to tell her that she was not looking well. She gave a weary little sigh and said she knew it.

Indeed, poor lady, it was apparent enough. She has taken of late to wearing her hair drawn up from her forehead over a roll—the effect of mouse-tints at which Nature is beginning to hint, being frankly helped out by powder. Everybody about Fernbank recognises that in some way this reform has altered the whole state of affairs. The very servant who comes to the door, or who brings in the tea-things, seems to carry herself in a different manner since the change has been made. Of course, it

is by no means a new fashion, but it was
not until the Dowager Countess of Thames-
Ditton brought it in person to Fernbank
that Mrs Albert could be quite sure of its
entire suitability. Up to that time it had
seemed to her a style rather adapted to
lady lecturers and the wives of men who
write : and though Mrs Albert has the very
highest regard for literature—quite dotes
on it, as she says—she is somewhat inclined to sniff at its wives.

We all feel that the change adds character
to Mrs Albert's face—or rather exhibits now
that true managing and resourceful temper,
which was formerly obscured and weakened
by a fringe. But the new arrangement has
the defects of its qualities. It does not
lend itself to tricks. The countenance
beneath it does not easily dissemble
anxiety or mask fatigue. And both were
written broadly over Mrs Albert's fine face.
" Yes," she said, " I know it."

The consoling suggestion that soon the
necessity of giving home-dinners to the
directors in her husband's companies would

have ended, and that then a few weeks out
of London, away somewhere in the air of the
mountains or the sea, would bring back all
her wonted strength and spirits, did no good.
She shook her head and sighed again.

" No," she said, " it isn't physical. That
is to say, it *is* physical, but the cause is
mental. It is over-worry."

"Of all people on earth—*you!*" I
replied reproachfully. "Why think of it
—a husband who is the dream of docile
propriety, a competency broadening each
year into a fortune, a home like this,
such servants, such appointments, such
a circle of admiring friends—and then
your daughters! Why, to be the mother
of such a girl as Ermyntrude———"

"Precisely," interrupted Mrs Albert.
" To be the mother of such a girl, as you
say. Little you know what it really
means! But, no—I know what you
were going to say—*please* don't! it is
too sad a subject."

I could do nothing but feebly strive
to look my surprise. To think of sadness

connected with tall, handsome, good-hearted Ermie, was impossible.

"You think I am exaggerating, I know," Mrs Albert went on. "Ah, you do not know!"

"Nothing could be more evident," I replied, "than that I don't know. I can't even imagine what on earth you are driving at."

Mrs Albert paused for a moment, and pushed the toe of her wee slipper meditatively back and forth on the figure of the carpet.

"Yes, I *will* tell you," she said at last. "You are such an old friend of the family that you are almost one of us. And besides, you are always sympathetic— so different from Dudley. Well, the point is this. You know the young man —Sir Watkyn's son—Mr Eustace Hump."

"I have met him here," I assented.

"Well, I doubt if you will meet him here any more," Mrs Albert said, impressively.

"The deprivation shall not drive me

to despair or drink," I assured her. " I
will watch over myself."

"I dare say you did not care much
for him," said Mrs Albert. "I know
Dudley didn't. But, all the same, he *was*
eligible. He is an only son, and his
father is a Baronet—an hereditary title—
and they are *rolling* in wealth. And
Eustace himself, when you get to know
him, has some very admirable qualities.
You know he *writes!*"

"I have heard him say so," I responded,
perhaps not over graciously.

" O, *regularly*, for a number of weekly
papers. It is understood that quite
frequently he gets paid—not of course
that that matters to him—but his asso-
ciations are distinctly literary. I have
always felt that with his tastes and connections his wife—granting of course that
she was the right kind of woman—might
at last set up a real literary *salon* in
London. We have wanted one so long,
you know."

"Have we?" I murmured listlessly,

striving all the while to guess what relation all this bore to the question of Ermyntrude. I built up in my mind a hostile picture of the odious Hump, with his shoulders sloping off like a German wine-bottle, his lean neck battlemented in high starched walls of linen, and his foolish conceited face—and leaped hopefully to the conclusion that Ermyntrude had rejected him. I could not keep the notion to myself.

"Well—has she sent him about his business?" I asked, making ready to beam with delight.

"No," said Mrs Albert, ruefully. "It never got to that, so far as I can gather—but at all events it is all over. I expect every morning now to read the announcement in the *Morning Post* that a marriage has been arranged between him and—and—Miss Wallaby!"

I sat upright, and felt myself smiling. "What!—the girl with the black ribbon round her neck?" I asked comfortably.

"It would be more appropriate round

her heart," remarked Mrs Albert, with
bitterness in her tone. "Why, do you
know? her mother, for all that she's
Lady Wallaby, hasn't an 'h' in her whole
composition."

"Well, neither has old Sir Watkyn
Hump," I rejoined pleasantly. "So it's a
fair exchange."

"Ah, but *he* can afford it," put in Mrs
Albert. "But the Wallabys—well, I
can only say that I had a right to look
for different treatment at *their* hands.
How, do you suppose, they would ever
have been asked to the Hon. Mrs
Coon-Alwyn's garden-party, or met Lady
Thames-Ditton, or been put in society
generally, if I had not taken an interest
in them? Why, that girl's father, old
Sir Willoughby Wallaby, was never anything but chief of police, or something like
that, out in some Australian convict
settlement. I *have* heard he was knighted
by mistake, but of course my lips are
sealed."

"I suppose they really have behaved
badly," I said, half interrogatively.

"Badly!" echoed the wrathful mother. "I will leave you to judge. It was done here, quite under my own roof. You know Miss Wallaby volunteered her services, and went down into the Retired Licensed Victuallers' Division of Surrey to electioneer for Sir Watkyn. Do you know, I never suspected anything. And then Miss Timby-Hucks, she went down also, but they rather cold-shouldered her, and she came back, and she told me things, and *still* I wouldn't believe it. Well then—three weeks ago—my Evening At Home—you were here—the Wallabys came as large as life, and that scheming young person manœuvred about until she got herself alone with Eustace and my Ermyntrude, and then she told her a scene she had witnessed during her recent election experiences. There was a meeting for Sir Watkyn at some place, I can't recall the name, and there were a good many of the other side there, and they hooted and shouted, and raised disturbance, until at last there was one speaker they would

not hear at all. All this that girl told
Ermyntrude seriously, and as if she were
overflowing with indignation. And then
she came to the part where the speaker
stood his ground and tried to make himself
heard, and the crowd yelled louder than
ever, and still he doggedly persisted—
and then someone threw a large vegetable
marrow, soft and very ripe, and it hit
that speaker just under the ear, and
burst all over him!"

"Ha-ha-ha!" I ejaculated. "The vegetable marrow in politics is new—full of
delightful possibilities and seeds—wonder
it has never been thought of before."

"Yes," said Mrs Albert, with a sigh.
"Ermyntrude also thought it was funny.
She has a very keen sense of humour—
quite too keen. *She* laughed, too!"

"And why not?" I asked.

"Why not?" demanded Mrs Albert,
with shining eyes. "Because the story
had been told just to trap her into
laughing—because—because the speaker
upon whom that unhappy vegetable
marrow exploded was—*Eustace Hump!*"

Containing Thoughts upon the Great Unknown, to which are added Speculations upon her Hereafter

IT is not often that I find the time to take part in Mrs Albert Grundy's Thursdays— the third and fifth Thursdays of each month, from 4 to 6.30 P.M.—but on a certain afternoon pleasant weather and the sense of long-accrued responsibility drew me to Fernbank.

It was really very nice, after one got there. Perhaps it would have been less satisfactory had escape from the drawing-room been a more difficult matter. In-side that formal chamber, with its blinds down-drawn to shield the carpet from the sun, the respectable air hung somewhat heavily about the assembled matronhood of Brompton and the Kensingtons. The

units in this gathering changed from time
to time—for Mrs Albert's circle is a large
and growing one—but the effect of the
sum remained much the same. The
elderly ladies talked about the amiability
and kindliness of the Duchess of Teck ;
and argued the Continental relationships
of the Duchesses of Connaught and Albany,
first into an apparently hopeless tangle
of *burgs* and *hausens* and *zollerns* and
sweigs, then triumphantly out again into
the bright daylight of well-ordered and
pellucid genealogy. The younger wives
spoke in subdued voices of more juvenile
Princesses on the lower steps of the throne,
with occasional short-winged flights across
the North Sea in imaginative search of
a suitable bride for the then unwedded
Duke of York, if an importation should
be found to be necessary—about which
opinions might in all loyalty differ. The
few young girls who sat dutifully here
beside their mammas or married sisters
talked of nothing at all, but smiled
confusedly and looked away whenever

another's glance, caught theirs—and, I
daresay, thought with decent humility
upon Marchionesses.

But outside, on the garden-lawn at the
rear of the house, the *Almanach de Gotha*
threw no shadow, and the pungent scent
of jasmine and lilies drove the leathery
odour of Debrett from the soft summer
air. The gentle London haze made
Whistlers and Maitlands of the walls
and roof-lines and chimney-pots beyond.
The pretty girls of Fernbank held court
here on the velvet grass, with groups of
attendant maidens from sympathetic Myrtle
Lodges and Cedarcrofts and Chestnut Villas
—selected homesteads stretching all the
way to remote West Kensington. They said
there was no one left in London. Why,
as I sat apart in the shade of the ivy overhanging the garden path, and watched
this out-door panorama of the Grundys'
friendships, it seemed as if I had never
comprehended before how many girls there
really were in the world.

And how sweet it was to look upon

these damsels, with their dainty sailor's
hats of straw, their cheeks of Devon cream
and damask, their tall and shapely forms,
their profiles of faultless classical delicacy !
What if, in time, they too must sit inside,
by preference, and babble of royalties and
the peerage, and politely uncover those
two aggressive incisors of genteel maturity
when they were asked to have a third
cup of tea ?   That stage, praise heaven,
should be many years removed.   We will
have no *memento mori* bones or tusks out
here in the sunlit garden—but only tennis
balls, and the inspiring chalk-bands on the
sward, and the noble grace of English girl-
hood, erect and joyous in the open air.

Much as I delighted in this spectacle,
it forced upon me as well a certain vague
sense of depression.   These lofty and
lovely creatures were strangers to me.   I
do not mean that their names were
unknown to me, or that I had not ex-
changed civil words with many of them,
or that I might not be presented to, and
affably received by, them all.   The feeling

was, rather, that if it were possible for me
to marry them all, we still to the end of
our days would remain strangers. I should
never know what to say to them; still
less should I ever be able to guess what
they were thinking.

The tallest and most impressive of all the
bevy—the handsome girl in the pale brown
frock with the shirt-front and jacketed
blouse, who stands leaning with folded
hands upon her racket like an indolent
Diana—why, I punted her about the whole
reach from Sunbury to Walton during the
better part of a week, only last summer,
not to mention sitting beside her at dinner
every evening on the houseboat. We were
so much together, in truth, that my friends
round about, as I came to know afterwards,
canvassed among themselves the prospect
of our arranging never to separate. Yet I
feel that I do not know this girl. We are
friends, yes; but we are not acquainted
with each other.

More than once—perhaps a dozen times
—in driving through the busier of London

streets, my fancy has been caught by this thing: a hansom whirling smartly by, the dark hood of which frames a woman's face —young, wistful, ivory-hued. It is like the flash exposure of a kodak—this bald instant of time in which I see this face, and comprehend that its gaze has met mine, and has burned into my memory a lightning picture of something I should not recognise if I saw it again, and cannot at all reproduce to myself, and probably would not like if I could, yet which leaves me with the feeling that I am richer than I was before. In that fractional throb of space there has been snatched an unrehearsed and unprejudiced contact of human souls—projected from one void momentarily to be swept forward into another; and though not the Judgment Day itself shall bring these two together again, they know each other.

Now that I look again at the goddess in the pale-brown gown, these unlabelled faces of the flitting hansoms seem by comparison those of familiar companions and intimates.

I get no sense of human communion from that serene and regular countenance, with its exquisite nose, its short upper-lip and glint of pearls along the bowed line of the mouth, its correctly arched brows and wide-open, impassive blue eyes.   I can see it with prophetic admiration out-queening all the others at Henley, or at Goodwood, or on the great staircase of Buckingham Palace.   I can imagine it at Monte Carlo, flushed a little at the sight of retreating gold ; or at the head of a great noble's table, coldly poised above satin throat and shoulders, and stirring no muscle under the free whisperings of His Excellency to the right.   I can conceive it in the Divorce Court, bearing with metallic equanimity the rude scrutiny of a thousand unlicensed eyes.   But my fancy wavers and fails at the task of picturing that face at my own fireside, with the light of the home-hearth painting the fulness of her rounded chin, and reflecting back from her glance, as we talk of men and books and things, the frank gladness of real comradeship.

F

But—tchut!—I have no fireside, and
the comrades I like best are playing half-
crown whist at the club ; and these are all
nice girls — hearty, healthful, handsome
girls, who can walk, run, dance, swim,
scull, skate, ride as no others have known
or dared to do since the glacial wave of
Christianity depopulated the glades and
dells of Olympus. They will mate after
their kind, and in its own good time along
will come a new generation of straight,
strong-limbed, thin-lipped, pink-and-white
girls, and of tow-headed, deep-chested lads,
their brothers—boys who will bully their
way through Rugby and Harrow, misspell
and misapprehend their way into the
Army, the Navy, and the Civil Service,
and spread themselves over the habitable
globe, to rule, through sheer inability to
understand, such Baboos and Matabele and
mere Irishry as Imperial destiny delivers
over to them.

The vision is not wholly joyous, as it
with diffidence projects itself beyond, into
that further space where new strange

other generations walk — the girls still
taller and more coldly tubbed, the boys
astride a yet more temerarious saddle of
dull dominion. Reluctant prophecy dis-
cerns beneath their considerable feet the
bruised fragments of many antique trifles
—the *bric-à-brac* of an extinct sentimental
fraction that had a sense of humour and
could spell—and, to please mamma, the fig-
leaves have quite overspread and hidden
the statues in their garden.   But power is
there, and empire ; they still more serenely
loom above the little foreign folks who
cook, and sing to harps and fiddles, and
paint for their amusement; such as it is
under their shaping, they possess the
earth.

So, as the sun goes down in the
Hammersmith heavens, I take off my hat,
and salute the potential mothers of the
New Rome.

*Glancing at some Modern Aspects of
Master John Gutenberg's ingenious
but Over-rated Invention*

IT was very pleasant thus to meet Uncle
Dudley in the Strand. Only here and
there is one who can bear that test. Whole
legions of our friends, decent and deeply
reputable people, fall altogether out of the
picture, so to speak, on this ancient yet
robust thoroughfare. They do very well
indeed in Chelsea or Highgate or the
Pembridge country, where they are at
home : there the surroundings fit them
to a nicety ; there they produce upon one
only amiable, or at the least, natural, impressions. But to encounter them in the
Strand is to be shocked by the blank in-
congruity of things. It is not alone that
they give the effect of being lost — of

wandering helplessly in unfamiliar places. They offend your perceptions by revealing limitations and shortcomings which might otherwise have been hidden to the end of time. You see suddenly that they are not such good fellows, after all. Their spiritual complexions are made up for the dim light which pervades the outskirts of the four-mile radius — and go to pieces in the jocund radiance of the Strand. It is flat presumption on their part to be ambling about where the ghosts of Goldsmith and Johnson walk, where Prior and Fielding and our Dick Steele have passed. Instinctively you go by, looking the other way.

It was quite different with Uncle Dudley. You saw at once that he belonged to the Strand, as wholly as any of our scorned and scornful sisters on its corners, competing with true insular doggedness against German cheeks and raddled accents; as fully as any of its indigenous loafers, hereditary in their riverside haunts from Tudor times, with their sophisticated joy in drink and dirt, their large self-confidence grinning through rags and sooty grime.   It seemed as if I had always associated Uncle Dudley with the Strand.

He was standing in contemplation before a brave window, wherein American cheese, Danish butter, Norwegian fish, Belgian eggs, German sausages, Hungarian bacon, French vegetables, Australian apples, and Algerian fruits celebrate the catholicity of the modern British diet.   He turned when I touched his shoulder, and drew my arm through his.

"Sir," said Uncle Dudley, "let us take a walk along the Strand to the Law Courts, where I conceive that the tide of human existence gets the worst of it with un-equalled regularity and dispatch."

On his way he told me that his gout had quite vanished, owing to his foresight in collecting a large store of the best medical advice, and then thoughtfully and with pains disregarding it all.   He demon-strated to me at two halting places that

his convalescence was compatible with rich
and strong drinks. He disclosed to me,
as we sauntered eastward, his purpose in
straying thus far afield.

"You know Mrs Albert is really a
kindly soul," he said. "It isn't in her to
keep angry. You remember how sternly
she swore that she and Fernbank had
seen the last of Miss Timby-Hucks. It
only lasted five weeks—and now, bless
me if the girl isn't more at home on our
backs than ever. She's shunted herself
off, now, into a new branch of journalism
—it seems that there are a good many
branches in these days."

"It has been noticed," I assented.

"She doesn't write any more," he explained, "that is, *for* the papers. She
goes instead to the Museum or somewhere,
and reads carefully every daily and weekly
journal, I believe, in England. Her business is to pick out possible libels in them
—and to furnish her employers, a certain
firm of solicitors, with a daily list of these.
They communicate with the aggrieved

people, notifying them that they *are* aggrieved, which they very likely would not otherwise have known, and the result is, of course, a very fine and spirited crop of litigation."

" Then that accounts for all the re-cent——"

" Perhaps not quite *all*," put in Uncle Dudley. " But the Timby-Hucks is both energetic · and vigilant, and she tells me she is doing splendidly. She is very enthusiastic about it, naturally. She says that while the money is, of course, an object, her real satisfaction is in the humanitarian aspects of her work."

" I am not sure that I follow," I said doubtingly.

" No, I didn't altogether myself at the start," said Uncle Dudley, " but as she explains it, it is very simple. You see business is in a bad way in London— worse, they say, than usual. The number of unemployed is something dreadful to think of, so I am told by those who have thought of it. There are many thousands of people with no food, no fire, no clothes to speak of. Most people are discouraged about this. They can't see how the thing can be improved. But Miss Timby-Hucks has a very ingenious idea. Why, she asks, do not all the Unemployed sue all the newspapers for libel? Do you catch the notion ? "

" By George ! " I exclaimed, " that is a bold, comprehensive thought ! "

" Yes, isn't it ? " cried Uncle Dudley. " I am immensely attracted by it. For one thing, it is so secure, so certain ! Broadly speaking, there are no risks at all. I suppose there has never yet been a case, no matter what its so-called merits, in which the English newspaper hasn't been cast in damages of some sort. Nobody is too humble or too shady to get a verdict against an editor or newspaper proprietor. Miss Timby-Hucks relates several most touching instances where the wolf was actually at the door, the children shoeless and hungry, the mother prostrated by drink, rain coming through the roof

and so on—and everything has been
changed to peace and contentment by the
happy thought of bringing a libel suit.
The father now wears a smile and a white
waistcoat ; the drains have been repaired ;
the little children, nicely washed and
combed, kick each other's shins with brand
new boots, and sing cheerfully beneath a
worsted-work motto of 'God bless our
Home!' I find myself much affected by
the thought."

" You had always a tender heart," I
responded. " I suppose there would be
no trouble about the Judges ? "

" Not the least in the world," said
Uncle Dudley, with confidence. " Of
course the Bench would have to be greatly
enlarged, but there need be no fear on
that score. There is a mysterious but
beneficent rule, my boy, which you can
always count upon in this making of
judges—no matter how hail-fellow-well-
met an eminent lawyer may be, no matter
how intimate his connection with newspapers, how large his indebtedness to them

for his career—the moment he gets on the Bench he catches the full, fine, old-crusted judicial spirit toward the Press. The scales fall with a bang from his eyes, and he sees the editor and newspaper proprietor as they really are—designing criminals, mercenary reprobates, social pests—to be lectured and bullied and put down. O, you may rely on the Judges! They are as safe as a new Liberal peer is to vote Tory."

"But the 'power of the Press'?" I urged. "If the newspapers combine in protest, and——"

"You talk at random!" said Uncle Dudley almost austerely. "I should say the most certain, the most absolutely reliable, element in the whole case is the fact that newspapers do not combine. Whenever one editor gets hit, all the others grin. One journal is mulcted in heavy damages: the rest have all a difficulty in dissembling their delight. You read in natural history that kites are given to falling upon one of their kind which gets wounded or decrepit,

and picking out its eyes.   Well, kites are
also made of newspapers."

"And juries ? " I began to ask.

" Here we are," remarked Uncle Dudley,
turning in toward the guarded portals of
the great hall.

" I have a friend among the attendants
here, a thoughtful and discerning man.   I
will learn from him where we may look
for the spiciest case.   He takes a lively
interest in the flaying of editors.   I believe he was once a printer.   He will tell
us where the axe gleams most savagely
to-day :   where we shall get the most
journalistic blood for our money.   You
were speaking of juries.   Just take a look
at one of them—if you are not afraid of
spoiling your luncheon—and you will see
that they speak for themselves.   They
regard all newspapers as public enemies—
particularly when the betting tips have
been more misleading than usual.   They
stand by their kind.   They 'give the poor
man a chance ' without hesitation, without
fail.   They are here to avenge the dis-

covery of movable types, and they do it.
Come with me, and witness the disem-
bowelling of a daily, the hamstringing of
a sub-editor—a publisher felled by the
hand of the Law like a bullock. Since
the bear-pits of Bankside were closed there
has been no such sport."

Unhappily, it turned out that none of
the Judges had come down to the Courts
that day. There was a threat of east wind
in the air. "You see, if they don't live
to a certain age they get no pensions,
and their heirs turn a key in the lock on
the old gentlemen in weather like this,"
explained Uncle Dudley, turning dis-
appointedly away.

Detailing certain Prudential Measures taken during the Panic incident to a Late Threatened Invasion

"I HOPE," said Mrs Albert, "that I am as free to admit my errors in judgment as another. Evidently there has been a mistake in this matter, and it is equally obvious that I am the one who must have made it. I did not need to have this pointed out to me, Dudley. What I looked to you for was advice, counsel, sympathy. You seem not to realise at all how important this is to me. A false step now may ruin everything—and you simply sit there and grin!"

" My dear sister," replied Uncle Dudley, smoothing his face, "the smile was involuntary. It shall not recur. I was only thinking of Albert's enthusiasm for the——"

"Yes, I know!" put in Mrs Albert; "for that girl with the zouave jacket——"

"*And* the scarlet petticoat,". prompted Uncle Dudley.

"*And* the crinoline," said the lady.

"O, he did not insist upon that. I recall his exact words. 'Whether this under-garment,' he said, 'be made of some stiff material like horsehair, or by means of steel hoops, is a mere question of detail.' No, Albert expressly kept an open mind on that point."

"I agree with you," remarked Mrs Albert coldly, "to the extent that he certainly does keep his mind on it. He has now reverted to the subject, I should think, at least twenty times. I am not so blind as you may imagine. I notice that that Mr Labouchere also keeps on referring, every week, to another girl in *her* zouave jacket, whom *he* remembers with equal fondness, apparently."

"Yes," put in Uncle Dudley, "those words about the 'stiff material like horsehair' *were* in *Truth*. I daresay Albert

simply read them there, and just uncon-
sciously repeated them.   We often do
inadvertent, unthinking things of that
sort."

Mrs Albert shook her head. "It is
nothing to me, of course," she said, "but I
cannot help feeling that the middle-aged
father of a family might concentrate his
thoughts upon something nobler, something higher, than the recollection of the
charms of a red petticoat, thirty years ago.
That is so characteristic of men.   They
cannot discuss a question broadly——"

" Think not ? " queried Uncle Dudley,
with interest. " You should listen at the
keyhole sometime, after you have led the
ladies out from dinner."

" I mean personally, in a general way.
They always particularise.   Albert, for example, allows all his views on this very important question to be coloured by the fact
that when he was a young man he admired
some girl in a short red Balmoral petticoat.
Whenever conversation touches upon any
phase of the whole subject of costume,

out he comes with his tiresome adulation
of that particular garment. Of course, I
ask no questions—I should prefer not to
be informed — I try not even to draw
inferences—but I notice that Ermyntrude
is beginning to observe the persistency with
which her father———"

"My good Emily," urged Uncle Dudley,
consolingly, "far back in the Sixties we
all liked that girl; we couldn't help ourselves—she was the only girl there was.
And we think of her fondly still—we old
fellows—because for us she was also the
last there was! When she went out, lo
and behold! we too had gone out, not to
come back any more. When Albert and
I babble about a scarlet petticoat, it is
only as a symbol of our own far-away
youth. O delicious vision!—the bright,
bright red, the skirt that came drooping
down over it, not hiding too much that
pretty little foot and ankle, the dear
zouave jacket moulding itself so delicately
to the persuasive encircling arm———"

"Dudley! I really must recall you to

G

yourself," said Mrs Albert. "We were
speaking of quite another matter. I am
in a very serious dilemma. First of all, as
I explained to you, to please the Hon. Mrs
Coon-Alwyn I became one of the Vice-
Presidents of the Friendly Divided Skirt
Association. You know how useful she can
be, in helping to bring Ermyntrude out
successfully. And of course everybody
knew that, even if we *did* have them *made*,
we should never *wear* them. That was
quite out of the question."

" And then ? " asked Uncle Dudley.

" Well, then, let me see—yes, next
came the Neo-Dress-Improver League. I
never understood what the object was, precisely ; it was a kind of secession from the
other, led by the Countess of Wimps, and
I needn't tell you that she is of the *utmost*
importance to us, and there was simply
nothing for me to do but to become a
Lady Patroness of *that*. You were in extremely nice company—there were seven or
eight ladies of title among the Patronesses,
our names all printed together in beautiful

little gilt letters—and you really weren't
committed to anything that I could make
out. No—*that* was all right. I should
do the same thing again, under the circumstances. No, the trouble came with the
Amalgamated Anti-Crinoline Confederacy.
That was where I was too hasty, I think."

"That's the thing with the protesting
post-cards, isn't it ? " inquired Uncle
Dudley.

"That very feature of it alone ought to
have warned me," Mrs Albert answered
with despondency. " My own better sense
should have told me that post-cards were
incompatible with selectness. But you see,
the invitations were sent out by the authoress
of *The Street-Sprinkler's Secret,* and that
gave me the impression that it was to be
literary — to represent Culture and the
Arts, you know; and that appealed to
me, of course, very strongly."

" I have always feared that your literary
impulses would run away with you," Uncle
Dudley declared gravely.

" It is my weak side ; I don't deny it,"

replied his sister. "Where letters and authorship, and that sort of thing, you know, are concerned, it is my nature to be sympathetic. And besides, the Dowager Lady Thames-Ditton was very pronounced in favour of the movement, and I *couldn't* fly in the face of that, could I ? I must say, though, that I had my misgivings almost from the first. Miss Wallaby told the Rev. Mr Grayt-Scott that a lady she knew had looked over quite a peck or more of the post-cards which came in one day, and they were nine-tenths of them from Earl's Court."

" Yes," remarked Uncle Dudley, " I think I have heard that the post-card reaches its most luxuriant state of literary usefulness in that locality. It was from that point that they tried to rush the Laureateship, you know."

" Well, you can imagine how I felt when I heard it. It is all well enough to be literary—nobody realises that more than I do—and it is all very well to be loyal— of course ! But one draws the line at

Earl's Court—at least, that part of it. I say frankly that it serves me right. I should have known better. One thing I cannot be too thankful for—Ermyntrude did not send a post-card. Some blessed instinct prompted me to tell her there was no hurry about it—that I did not like to see young girls too forward in such matters. And now—why—who knows—Dudley! I have an idea! Ermie shall join the Crinoline Defence League!"

"I see—the family will hedge on the crinoline issue. Capital!"

"You know, after all, we may have to wear them. It's quite as likely as not. The old Duchess of West Ham is President of the League, and she is very influential in the highest quarters. Her Grace, I understand, *is* somewhat bandy, but she has always maintained the strictest Christian respectability, and her action in this matter will count for a great deal. Just think, if she should happen to take a fancy to Ermyntrude! That Miss Wallaby has thrust herself forward till she is actually

a member of the Council, and she is going
to deliver an address on 'The Effect of
Modesty on National Morals.' She told
our curate that at one of the meetings of
the Council she came within an ace of
being introduced to the Duchess herself.
Now surely, if *she* can accomplish all this,
Ermie ought to be able to do still more.
Tell me, Dudley, what do *you* think ? "

"I think," replied Uncle Dudley mus-
ingly, "I think that the scarlet petticoat,
with the zouave jack———"

Mrs Albert interrupted him with sternness. "Don't you see," she demanded,
"that if it *does* come, the dear girl will
share in the credit of bringing it in, and if
it doesn't come, I shall have the advantage
of having helped to stave it off. Which-
ever side wins, there we are."

Uncle Dudley rose, and looked thoughtfully out upon the fog, and stroked his large
white moustache in slow meditation. "Yes
—undoubtedly," he said at last, "there we
are."

*Dealing with the Deceptions of Nature,
and the Freedom from Illusion
Inherent in the Unnatural*

THERE was once a woman—obviously a
thoughtful woman — who remarked that
she had noticed that if she managed to
live till Friday, she invariably survived
the rest of the week.   I did not myself
know this philosopher, who is preserved to
history in one of Roscoe Conkling's speeches,
but her discovery always recurs to me about
this time of year, when February begins to
disclose those first freshening glimpses of
sunlight and blue skies to bleared, fog-
smudged and shivering London.   Aha! if
we have won thus far, if we have contrived
to get to February, then we shall surely see
the Spring.   At least the one has heretofore involved the other—and there is con-

fident promise in the smile of a noon-day
once more able to cast a shadow, albeit the
teeth of the east wind gleam close behind
that smile.

It was a day for a walk—no set and
joyous rural tramp, indeed, with pipe and
wallet, and a helpful spring underfoot in
the clean hard roadway, and an honest,
well-balanced stick for the bell-ringing
gentry who shall come at you on wheels
from behind—but just an orderly, contem-
plative urban ramble, brisk enough for
warmth, but with no hurry, and above all
no destination.   And it was a day, moreover, for letting one's fellow-creatures pass
along with scant notice—a winter-ridden,
shuffling, mud-stained company these, conscious of being not at all worth examination
—and for giving eye instead to the house-
fronts in the sunshine, and radiant chimney-
pots and tiles above them, and the signs of
blessed, unaccustomed blue still further up.
There was, it is true, an undeniable dis-
proportion between the inner look of these
things, and this gladness of the heart be-

cause of them.   Glancing more closely, one could see that they were not taking the sun seriously, and, for their own part, were expecting more fogs next week.   And farther westward, when stucco, brick, and stone gave way to park-land, it was apparent at sight that the trees were flatly incredulous.

They say that in Ireland, where the mildness of climate has in the past prompted many experiments with exotic growths, the trees not really indigenous to the island never learn sense, but year after year are gulled by this February fraud into gushing expansively forth with sap and tender shoots, only to be gripped and shrivelled by the icy after-hand of March. The native tree, however, knows this trick of old, and greets the sham Spring with a distinctive, though well-buttoned-up wink. In Kensington Park region one couldn't be sure that the trees really saw the joke. It is not, on the whole, a humourous neighbourhood.   But at all events they were not to be fooled into premature buds

and sprouts and kindred signs of silliness.
Every stiffly exclusive drab trunk rising
before you, every section of the brown
lacework of twigs up above, seemed to
offer a warning advertisement: "No connection with the sunshine over the way!"

Happily the flower-beds exhibited more
sympathy. Up through the mould brave
little snowdrops had pushed their pretty
heads, and the crocuses, though with their
veined outer cloaks of sulphur, mauve, and
other tints still wrapped tight about them,
wore almost a swaggering air to show how
wholly they felt at home. Emboldened
by this bravado, less confident fellows were
peeping forth, though in such faltering
fashion that one could scarcely tell which
was squill, which narcissus or loitering
jonquil. Still, it was good to see them.
They too were glad that they had lived
till February, because after that comes the
Spring.

And it was better still, as I turned to
stroll on, to behold coming toward me
down the path, with little swinging step,

and shapely head well up in air, none
other than our Ermyntrude.

I say "our" because—it is really absurd
to think of it—it seems only a few months
ago since she was a sprawling tom-boy
sort of a little girl, who sat on my knee
and listened with her mouth open to my
reminiscences of personal encounters with
unicorns and the behemoth of Holy Writ.
She must be now—by George! she *is*—
not a minute under two-and-twenty. And
that means—*hélas!* it undoubtedly means
—that I am getting to be an old boy
indeed. At Christmas-tide—I recall it
now—Mrs Albert spoke of me as the
oldest friend of the family. It sounded
kindly at the time, and I had a special
pleasure in the smile Ermyntrude wore as
she, with the others, lifted her glass towards me. I won't say what vagrant
thoughts and ambitions that smile did
not raise in my mind—and, lo! they
were toasting me as an amiable elderly
friend of the Fernbank household. No
wonder I am glad to have lived till
February!

Ermyntrude had a roll of music in her hands. There was a charming glow on her cheeks, and a healthy, happy, sparkle in her eyes. She stopped short before me, with a little exclamation of not displeased surprise !

"Why, how nice to run upon you like this," she said, in high spirits. "We thought you must have gone off to the Riviera, or Algiers, or somewhere — for your cold, you know. Mamma was speaking of you only yesterday—hoping that you were taking care of yourself."

"Had I a cold ?" I asked absently. The air had grown chillier. We walked along together, and she let me carry the music.

"O—you haven't heard," she exclaimed suddenly, "such news as I have for you ! You couldn't ever guess ! "

" Is it something about crinoline ? " I queried. " Your mother was telling me—— "

" Rubbish ! " said Ermyntrude gaily. " I'm engaged ! "

The wind had really got round into the East, and I fastened my coat at the collar. "I am sure"—I remarked at last—"I'm sure I congratulate — the happy young man. Do I know him?"

"I hardly think so," she replied. "You see, it's—it's what you might call rather sudden. We haven't known him ourselves very long — that is, intimately. You may have heard his name — the Honourable Knobbeleigh Jones. It's a very old family though the title is somewhat new. His father is Lord Skillyduff, you know."

"The shipping man?" I said, wearily.

"Yes. He and papa are together on some board or other. That is how we came to know them. Papa says he never saw such business ability and sterling worth combined in one man before—I'm speaking of the father, you know. He began life in quite a small way, with just a few ships that he rented, or something like that. Then there was a war on some coast in Africa or Australia—it begins

with an **A**, I know—oh, *is* there a place
called Ashantee?—yes, that's it—and he
got the contract to take out four shiploads
of hay to our troops—it would be for their
horses, wouldn't it?"

"Yes : the asses connected with the
military branch are needed at home—
or at least are kept there."

"Well, after he started, he got orders
to stop at some place and wait for other
orders. He did so, and he waited four
years and eight months. Those orders
never came. The hay all rotted, of
course : the ships almost moulded away :
I daresay some of the crew died of old
age—But Mr Jones never stirred from his
post. Finally, some English official came
on him by accident—quite ! and so he
was recalled. Papa says very few men
would have shown such tenacity of purpose and grasp of the situation. Mamma
says his fidelity to duty was magnificent."

"Magnificent—yes," I commented ; "but
it wasn't war."

"Oh, bless you ! there *was* no war

then," explained Ermyntrude. "The war
had been ended for *years.* And all that
while the pay for shipping that hay had
been going on, so that the Government
owed him—I think it was £45,000. Of
course he got more contracts, and then he
was made a baronet, and could build his
own ships; and now he is a lord, and
papa says the War Office would be quite
helpless without him."

"And the son," I asked; "what does
he do?"

"Why, nothing, of course!" said Ermyntrude, lifting her pretty brows a little in
surprise. "He is the eldest son."

"I didn't know but he might have gone
in for the Army, or Parliament, or something," I explained weakly: "just to
occupy his mind."

She smiled to herself—somewhat grimly,
I thought. "No," she said, assuming a
serious face, "he says doing things is all
rot, if you aren't obliged to do them. Of
course, he goes in for hunting and shooting
and all that, and he has a houseboat and

a yacht, and one year he was in the All-
Slumpshire eleven, but that was too much
bother.   He hates bother."

We had come out upon the street now,
and walked for a little in silence.

"Ermie," I said at last, "you mustn't
be annoyed with me—this is one of my
sentimental days, and you know as an old
friend of the family I've a certain right of
free speech—but this doesn't seem to me
quite good enough.   A girl like you—
beautiful and clever and accomplished,
knowing your way about among books,
and with tastes above the ruck—there
ought to be a better outlook for you
than this! I know that type of young
man, and he isn't in your street at all.
Come now!" I went on, gathering courage,
"look me in the face if you can, and tell
me that you honestly love this young man,
or that you really respect his father, or
that you candidly expect to be happy.   I
defy you to do it!"

I was wrong.   Ermyntrude did look me
in the face, squarely and without hesita-

tion. She halted for the moment to do
so, and her gaze, though not unkindly, was
full of serious frankness.

"There is one thing I do expect," she
said, calmly. "I expect to get away from
Fernbank."

Suggesting Considerations possibly heretofore Overlooked by Commentators upon the Laws of Property

"You will find Dudley up in what he calls his library," said Mrs Albert in the hallway. "I'm *so* sorry I must go out —but he'll be glad to see you. And— let me entreat you, don't give him any encouragement!"

"What!" I cried, "encourage Uncle Dudley? Oh—never, never!"

"No, just be firm with him," Mrs Albert went on. "Say that it mustn't be thought of for a moment. And Oh— by the way—it's as well to warn you: *don't* ask him what he did it for! It seems that every one asks him that—and he gets quite enraged about it now, when that particular question is put. As like as

not he'd throw something at you." She
spoke earnestly, in low, impressive tones.

"Wild horses should not drag it from
me," I pledged myself. "I will not encourage him : I will not enrage him; I
swear not to ask him what he did it for.
But—if you don't mind—could I, so to
speak, bear the shock of learning what it
is that he *has* done ?"

"You haven't heard?" Mrs Albert asked,
glancing up at me, with an astonished face,
as I stood on the stairs. When I shook
my head, she put out her hand to the latch,
and opened the door, as if to heighten the
dramatic suspense. Then she turned and
looked me in the eye with solemn intent-
ness. "What has he done ? " she echoed
in a hollow voice: "You go upstairs and
see ! "

The door closed behind her, and I made
my way noiselessly, two steps at a time,
to the floor above. Some vague sense of
disaster seemed to brood over the silent,
half-lighted stairway and the deserted land-
ing. I knocked at Uncle Dudley's door

—almost prepared to find my signal un-
answered. But no, his voice came back,
cheerily enough, and I entered the room.

"Oh, it's you!" said my friend, rising
from his chair. "Glad to see you,"—and
we shook hands. Standing thus, I found
myself staring into his face with a rude
and prolonged fixity of gaze, under which
he first smiled—a strange, unwholesome
sort of smile—then flushed a little, then
scowled and averted his glance.

"Great heavens!" I exclaimed at last.
"Why, man alive, what on earth possessed
you to—"

"Come now!" broke in Uncle Dudley,
with peremptory sternness. "Chuck it!"

"Yes—I know"—I stammered halt-
ingly along—"I promised I wouldn't ask
you—but—"

"But the original simian instincts
triumph over your resolutions, eh?" said
my friend, crustily. "Yes, I know. I've
had pretty nearly a week of it now.
That question has been asked me, I
estimate, somewhere about six hundred

and seventy-eight times since last Thursday. It's only fair to you to tell you that I have registered a vow to hit the next man who asks me that fool of a question—'What did you do it for?' —straight under his left ear. I probably saved your life by interrupting you."

Though the words were fierce, there was a marked return of geniality in the tone. I took the liberty of putting a hand over Uncle Dudley's shoulder, and marching him across to the window.

"Let's have a good look at you," I said.

"I did it myself; I did it with my little hatchet; I did it because I wanted to; I had a right to do it; I should do it again if the fit struck me——" Thus, with mock gravity, Uncle Dudley ran on as I scrutinised his countenance in the strong light. "And furthermore," he added, "I don't care one single hurrah in Hades whether you like it or not."

"I think on the whole," I mused aloud —"yes, I think I rather do like it—now that I accustom myself to it."

Uncle Dudley's face brightened on the instant. "Do you really?" he exclaimed, and beamed upon me. In spite of his professed indifference to my opinion, it was obvious that I had pleased him.

"Sit down," he said—"there are the matches behind you—hope these aren't too green for you. Yes, my boy, I created quite a flutter in the hen-yard, I can tell you. Did my sister tell you?—she nearly fainted, and little Amy burst out boohooing as if she'd lost her last friend. When you come to think of it, old man, it's really too ridiculous, you know."

"It certainly has its grotesque aspects," I admitted.

Uncle Dudley looked up sharply, as if suspecting some ironical meaning in my words. "You really do think it's an improvement?" he asked, with a doubtful note in his voice.

"Of course, it makes a tremendous change," I said, diplomatically, "and the novelty tends perhaps to confuse judg-

ment : but I must confess the result is—
is, well, very interesting."

My friend did not look wholly satisfied.
"It shows what stupid people we are," he
went on in a dogmatic way.   "Why, the
way they've gone on, you'd think I had no
property rights in the thing at all—that I
was merely a trustee for it—bound to give
an account to every Tom-Dick-and-Harry
who came along and had nothing better
to occupy his mind with.   And then that
eternal, vacuous, woollen-brained 'What
did you do it for?'   Oh, that's got to be
too sickening for words!   And the con-
founded familiarity of the whole thing!
Why, hang me, if even the little Jew cigar
dealer down on the corner didn't feel
entitled to pass what he took to be some
friendly remarks on the subject. 'Vy,'
he said, 'if I could say vidout vlattery,
vot a haddsobe jeddlebad you ver, and
vy did you do dot by yourself?'   It gets
on a man's nerves, you know, things like
that."

"But hasn't anyone liked the change?"
I asked.

Uncle Dudley sighed. "That's the
worst of it," he said, dubiously. "Only
two men have said they liked it—and
it happens that they are both persons
of conspicuously weak intellect. That's
rather up against me, isn't it? But on
the other hand, you know, people who are
silliest about everything else always get
credit for knowing the most about art and
beauty and all that. Perhaps in such
a case as this, I daresay their judgment
might be better than all the others. And
after all, what do *I* care? That's the
point I make : that it's *my* business and
nobody else's. If a man hasn't got a
copyright in his own personal appearance,
why there is no such thing as property.
But instead of recognising this, any fellow
feels free to come up and say : 'You look
like an unfrocked priest,' or 'Hullo!
another burglar out of work,' and he's
quite surprised if you fail to show that
you're pleased with the genial brilliancy of
his remarks. I don't suppose there is
any other single thing which the human

race lapses into such rude and insolent meddlesomeness over as it does over this."

"It *is* pathetic," I admitted—"but—but it'll soon grow again."

Uncle Dudley laughed a bitter laugh. "By Jove," he cried, "I've more than half a mind not to let it. It would serve 'em right if I didn't. Why, do you know—you'd hardly believe it! My sister had a dinner party on here for Saturday night, and after I'd—I'd done it—she cancelled the invitations—some excuse about a family loss—a bereavement, my boy. Well, you know, treatment of that sort puts a man on his mettle. I'm entitled to resent it. And besides—you know—of course it does make a great change—but somehow I fancy that when you get used to it—come now—the straight griffin, as they say—what do *you* think?"

"I'm on oath not to encourage you," I made answer.

"There you have it!" cried Uncle Dudley: "the old tyrannical conspiracy

against the unusual, the individual, the
true! Let nobody dare to be himself!
Let us have uniformity, if all else perishes.
The frames must be alike in the Royal
Academy, that's the great thing; the
pictures don't matter so much. You see
our women-folk now, this very month,
getting ready to case themselves in ugly
hoops which they hate, at the bidding of
they know not whom, because, if they did
not, the hideous possibility of one woman
being different from another woman would
darken the land. A man is not to be
permitted the pitiful privilege of seeing his
own mouth, not even once in fifteen
years, simply because it temporarily
inconveniences the multitude in their
notions as to how he is in the habit of
looking! What rubbish it is!"

"It *is* rubbish," I assented—"and you
are talking it. Your sister who fainted,
your niece who wept, your friends who
averted their gaze in anguish, the hordes
of casual jackasses who asked why you
did it, the kindly little Jew cigar man who

broke forth in lamentations—these are the world's jury. They have convicted you— sorrowfully but firmly. You yourself, for all your bravado, realise the heinousness of your crime. You are secretly ashamed, remorseful, penitent. I answer for you— you will never do it again."

"And yet it isn't such a bad mouth, either," mused Uncle Dudley, with a lingering glance at the mirror over the mantel. "There is humour, delicacy of perception, affection, gentleness—ever so many nice qualities about it which were all hidden up before. The world ought to welcome the revelation—and it throws stones instead. Ah well!—pass the matches—let us yield gracefully to the inevitable! It shall grow again."

"Mrs Albert will be so glad," I re- marked.

Narrating the Failure of a Loyal Attempt to Circumvent Adversity by means of Modern Appliances

"IF his name was Jabez, why weren't we told so, I'd like to know?" demanded Mrs Albert of me, with a momentary flash in her weary glance. "What right had the papers to go on calling him J. Spencer, year after year, while he was deluding the innocent, and fattening upon the bodies of his dupes? To be sure, now that the mask is off, and he has fled, they speak of him always as Jabez. Why didn't they do it before, while honest people might still have been warned? But no—they never did— and now it's too late—too late!"

The poor lady's voice broke pathetically upon this reiterated plaint. She bowed her head, and as I looked with pained sympathy upon the drooping angle of her proud face, I could see the shadows about her lips quiver.

A sad tale indeed it was, to which I had been listening—here in a lonesome corner of the cloistral, dim-lit solitude of the big drawing-room at Fernbank. It was not a new story. Kensington has known it by heart for a generation. Bloomsbury learned it earlier, and before that it was familiar in Soho—away off in the old days when the ruffling gentry of Golden Square fought for the chance of buying ingenious John Law's South Sea scrip. And even then, the experience was an ancient and half-forgotten memory of Bishopsgate and the Minories. It was the old, old tragedy of broken fortunes.

Mrs Albert was clear that it began with the Liberator troubles. I had my own notion that Mr Albert Grundy was skating on thin ice before the collapse of the building societies came. However that may be, there was no doubt whatever that the cumulative Australian disasters had finished

the business. There were melancholy details in her recital which I lack the courage
to dwell upon. The horse and brougham
were gone ; the lease of Fernbank itself
was offered for sale, with possession before
Michaelmas, if desired ; Ermyntrude's en-
gagement was as good as off.

"It won't be a bankruptcy," said Mrs
Albert, lifting her face and resolutely
winking the moisture from her lashes.
"We shall escape that — but for the
moment at least I must abandon my
position in society. Dudley is over to-day
looking at a small place in Highgate,
although Albert thinks he would prefer
Sydenham. My own feeling is that some
locality from which you could arrive by
King's Cross or St Pancras would be best.
One never meets anybody one knows there.
Then, when matters adjust themselves
again, as of course they will, we could
return here—to this neighbourhood, at
least—and just mention casually having
been out at our country place—on the
children's account, of course. And Floribel
is delicate, you know."

"Oh well, then," I said, trying to put buoyance into my tone, "it isn't so bad after all. And you feel—Albert feels— quite hopeful about things coming right again?"

My friend's answering nod of affirmation had a certain qualifying dubiety about it. "Yes, we're hopeful," she said. "But a fortnight ago, I felt positively sanguine. Nobody ever worked harder than I did to deserve success, any way. I only failed through gross treachery—and that, too, at the hands of the very people of whom I could never, *never* have believed it. When you find the aristocracy openly actuated by mercenary motives, as I have done this past month, it almost makes you ask what the British nation is coming to!"

"Dear me!" I exclaimed, "is it as bad as that?"

"You shall judge for yourself," said Mrs Albert gravely. "You know that I organ- ised—quite early in the Spring—the Loyal Ladies' Namesake Committee of Kensing- ton. I do not boast in saying that I really

organised it, quite from its beginnings.
The idea was mine; practically all the
labour was mine. But when one is toiling
to realise a great ideal like that, one
frequently loses sight of small details. I
ought to have known better—but I took a
serpent to my bosom. I was weak enough
to associate with me in the enterprise that
monument of duplicity and interested motives—the Hon. Mrs Coon-Alwyn. Why,
she hadn't so much as an initial letter to
entitle her to belong—— "

"I am not sure that I follow you," I
put in. "Ladies' Namesake Committee—
initial letter—I don't seem to grasp the
idea."

"It's perfectly simple," explained Mrs
Albert. "The idea was that all the ladies
—our set, you know—whose name was
'May' should combine in subscribing for
a present."

"But your name is Emily," I urged,
thoughtlessly.

"Oh, we weren't exactly literal about
it," said Mrs Albert; "we *couldn't* be, you

know. It would have shut out some of our very best people. But I came very near the standard, indeed. My second name is Madge. You take the first two letters of that, and the 'y' from Emily, and there you have it. Oh, I assure you, very few came even as near it as that— and as I said to Dudley at the time, if you think of it, even *her* name isn't *really* May. It's only a popular contraction. But that Hon. Mrs Coon-Alwyn, she had no actual right whatever to belong. Her names are Hester Winifred Edith. She hasn't even one *letter* right!"

"Ah, that was indeed treachery!" I ejaculated.

"Oh, no, that. was not what I referred to," Mrs Albert set me right. "Of course, I was aware of her names. I had seen them in the 'Peerage' for years. It was what she did after her entrance that covers her with infamy. But I will narrate the events in their order. First, we collected £1100. Of course, our own contribution was not large, but Ermyntrude and I

I

hunted the various church registers—we
don't speak of it, but even the Noncon-
formist ones we went through—and we got
a tremendous number of Christian names
more or less what was desired, and our
circulars were sent to *every one*, far and
near. As I said, we raised quite £1100.
Then there came the question of the gift."

Mrs Albert uttered this last sentence
with such deliberate solemnity that I
bowed to show my consciousness of its
importance.

"Yes," she went on, "the selection of
the gift. Now I had in mind a most
appropriate and useful present. Have you
heard of the Oboid Oil Engine ? No ?
Well, it is an American invention, and has
been brought over here by an American,
who has bought the European rights from
the inventor. He is in the next building
to Albert, in the City, and they meet almost
every day at luncheon, and have struck up
quite a friendship. He has connections
which might be of the *utmost* importance
to Albert, and if Albert could only have

been of service to him in introducing this
engine, there is literally *no telling* what
might not have come of it.   Albert does
not *say* that a partnership would have
resulted, but I can read it in his face."

"But would an oil engine have been—
under the circumstances—you know what
I mean——" I began.

"Oh, *most* suitable !" responded Mrs
Albert with conviction.   "It is really, it
seems, a very surprising piece of machinery.
After it's once bought, the cheapness of
running it is simply *absurd*.   It does all
sorts of things at no expense worth men-
tioning—anything you want it to do.   It
appears that if it had been invented at
that time, the pyramids in Egypt could
have been built by it for something like
130 per cent. less than their cost is estimated to have been—or something like that.
Oh, it is quite extraordinary, I assure you.
Albert says he could stand and watch it
working for hours—especially if he had an
interest in the company."

"But I hadn't heard that there were

any new pyramid plans on just now—
although, when I think of it, Shaw-Lefevre
did have some Westminster Abbey project
which——"

"No, no!" interrupted Mrs Albert.
"One of the engine's greatest uses is in
agriculture. It does *everything*—threshes,
garners, mows, milks—or no, not that, but
almost *everything*. No self-respecting
farmer, they say, dreams of being without
one—that is, of course, if he knows about
it. You can see what it would have
meant, if one had been thus publicly introduced on the princely farm at Sandring-
ham. All England would have rung with
demands for the Oboid—and Albert feels
sure that the American man would have
been grateful—and—and—then perhaps
we need never have left Fernbank at all."

My poor friend shook her head mourn-
fully at the thought.

"And the Hon. Mrs Coon-Alwyn?" I
asked.

The fire came back into Mrs Albert's
eye. "That woman," she said, with bitter

calmness, "was positively not ashamed to
intrude her own mercenary and self-seeking
designs upon this loyal and purely patriotic
association.   Why, she did it almost openly.
She intrigued behind my back with whole
streetsful of people that one would hardly
know on ordinary occasions, paid them calls
in a carriage got up for the occasion with a
bright new coat of arms, made friends with
them, promised them heaven only knows
what, and actually secured nineteen votes to
my three for the purchase of a mouldy old
piece of tapestry—something about Richard
III and Oliver Cromwell meeting on the
battlefield, I think the subject is—which
belonged to her husband's family.   Of
course, my lips are sealed, but I have been
told that at Christie's it would hardly have
fetched £100.   I say nothing myself, but
I can't prevent people drawing certain
deductions, can I ?   And when I reflect
also that her two most active supporters in
this nefarious business were Lady Thames-
Ditton — whose financial difficulties are
notorious—and the Countess of Wimps—

whose tradespeople—well, we won't go into
that—it does force one to ask whether the
fabric of British society is not being under-
mined at its very top.   In this very day's
paper I read that the Hon. Mrs Coon-
Alwyn has hired a yacht, and will spend
the summer in Norwegian waters—while
we—we——— "

The door opened, and we made out
through the half-light the comfortable figure
of Uncle Dudley.   He was mopping his
brow, and breathed heavily from his long
walk as he advanced.

" Well ?" Mrs Albert asked, in a saddened
and subdued tone, " Did you see the
place ? "

" There are five bedrooms on the two
upper floors," he made answer, " but there's
no bath-room, and the bus doesn't come
within four streets of the house."

Introducing Scenes from a Foreign Country, and also conveying Welcome Intelligence, together with some Instruction

IT was at a little village perched well up on one of the carriage-roads ascending the Brocken, a fortnight or so ago, that I received a wire from Uncle Dudley. It was kind of him to think of it—all the more as he had good news to tell. "Family lighted square on their feet," was what the message said, and I was glad to gather from this that the Grundys had weathered their misfortunes, and that Mrs Albert was herself again.

The thought was full of charm. It seemed as if I had never realised before how fond I was of these good people. In sober fact, I dare say that I had not dwelt

much upon their woes during my holiday.
But now, with this affectionately thoughtful telegram addressing me as their
oldest friend, the one whom they wished
to be the first to share the joy of their
rescued state, it was easy enough to make
myself believe that my whole vacation had
been darkened with brooding over their
unhappiness.

It had not occurred to me before, but
that was undoubtedly why I had not liked
the Harz so much this year as usual. Now
that I thought of it, walking down the
birch-lined footpath towards the hamlet
and the telegraph office, the place seemed
to have gone off a good deal. In other
seasons, before the spectre of cholera flooded
its sylvan retreats with an invading horde
of Hamburgers, the Harzwald had been my
favourite resort. I had grown to love its
fir-clad slopes, its shadowed glens, its atmo-
sphere of prehistoric myth and legend, as
if I were part and product of them all.
Its people, too, had come much nearer to
my breast than any other Germans ever

could. I had enjoyed being with them just because they were what the local schoolmaster disdainfully declared them to be—*Erdzertrümmerungsprozeszunbekanntevolk*—that is to say, people entirely ignorant of the scientific theories about geological upheavals and volcanic formations, and so able cheerfully to put their trust in the goblins who reared these strange boulders in fantastic piles on every hill top, and to hear with good faith the shouts of the witches as they bounded over the *Hexentanzplatz*. Last year it had seemed even worth the added discomfort of the swarming Hamburgers to be again in this wholesome, sweet-aired primitive place.

But this year—I saw now clearly as I looked over Uncle Dudley's message once more—it had not been so pleasant. The hotel boy, Fritzchen, whom I had watched year after year with the warmth of a fatherly well-wisher—smiling with satisfaction at his jovial countenance, his bustling and competent ways, and his comical attempts at English—had this

season swollen up into a burly and con-
sequential lout, with a straw - coloured
sprouting on his upper-lip, and a military
manner. They called him Fritz now, and
he gave me beer out of the old keg after I
had heard the new one tapped.

The evening gatherings of the villagers
in the hotel, too, were not amusing as they
once had been. The huge lion-maned and
grossly over-bearded *Kantor*, or music-
master, who came regularly at nightfall to
thump on the table with his bludgeon-like
walking stick, to roar forth impassioned
monologues on religion and politics, and to
bellow ceaselessly at Fritzchen for more
beer, had formerly delighted me. This
time he seemed only a noisy nuisance, and
the half-circle of grave old retired foresters
and middle-aged *Jäger* officers who sat
watching him over their pipes, striving
vainly now and again to get in a word
edgewise about the auctions of felled trees
in the woods, or the mutinous tendencies of
the charcoal-burners, presented themselves
in the light of tiresome prigs. If they had

been worth their salt, I felt, they would
long ago have brained the Kantor with
their stoneware mugs. Even as I walked
I began to be conscious that a three weeks'
stay in the Harz was a good deal of time,
and that the remaining third would certainly hang on my hands.

By the time I reached the telegraph
station I had my answer to Uncle Dudley
ready in my mind. He liked the forcible
imagery of Australia and the Far West; and
I would speak to him at this joyful juncture
after his own heart. It seemed that I
could best do this by giving him to understand that I was celebrating his news—that
I was, in one of his own phrases, " painting
the town red." It required some ingenuity
to work this idea out right, but I finally
wrote what appeared to answer the purpose :—" *Brocken und Umgebung sind
roth gemalen* "—and handed it in to the
man at the window.

He was a young man with close-cropped
yellow hair and spectacles, holding his chin
and neck very stiff in the high collar of his

uniform. He glanced over my despatch, at
first with careless dignity. Then he read
it again attentively. Then he laid it on
the table, and bent his tight-buttoned form
over it as well as might be in a severe and
prolonged scrutiny. At last he raised
himself, turned a petrifying gaze on through
his glasses at me, and shook his head. ·

" It is not true," he said. " Some one
has you deceived."

" But," I tried to explain to him, with
the little German that I knew scattering
itself in all directions in the face of this
crisis, " it is a figure of speech, a joke,
a——— "

The telegraph man stared coldly at my
luckless despatch, and then at me. " You
would wish to state to your friend, perhaps," he suggested, " that they seem as if
they had been coloured with red, owing to
the change in the leaves."

" No, no," I put in. " It must be that
they *have* been painted, *are* painted, or he
will not me understand."

" But, my good sir," retorted the operator

with emphasis, " they are *not* painted !
From the door gaze you forth ! What
make you with this nonsense, that Brocken
and vicinity are red painted ? "

" Well, then," I said wearily, oppressed
by the magnitude of the task, " I don't
know how to word it myself, but you can
fix it for me. Just say that I am *going*
to paint them red—that will do just as
well.

" But you shall not ! It is forbidden ! "
exclaimed the official, holding himself like
a poker, and glaring vehemence through
his glasses. " It is strongly forbidden !
When you one brush-mark shall make,
quick to the prison go you. In Germany
have we for natural beauty respect—also
laws."

Reluctantly, but of necessity, I abandoned metaphor, and in a humble spirit
telegraphed in English to Uncle Dudley
at his club that I was very glad. Even as
my pen clung in irresolution on the paper
over this word " glad," the impulse rose
in me to add : " Tired of Harz. Am
returning immediately."

"When the same here is," remarked the
operator, moodily studying the unknown
words, "in Brunswick stopped it will
be."

I translated it for him, and added, "I
go from here home, to be where officials
their own business mind."

He nodded, not unamiably, and replied
as he handed me out my change : "Yes, I
know : England. So well their own business there officials mind, that Balfour to
Argentina easily comes."

Walking up the hillside again, already
quite captive to the fascination of the
morrow's homeward flight, I met at the
turn of the path a family party—father,
mother, and two girls in the younger teens
—seated along the rocky siding, and
gazing with a common air of dejection
upon a portentous row of bags and port-
manteaus at their feet. The notion that
they were Hamburgers died still-born.
Nothing more obviously un-German than
these wayfarers was ever seen.

"I hope, sir," the man spoke up as I

approached, " that I am right in presuming
that you speak English ! "

I bowed assent, and even as I did so,
recognised him.   " I hope *I* am right," I
answered, " in thinking that I have met
you before—at Mr Albert Grundy's in
London—you are the American gentleman
with the Oboid Oil Engine, are you not ? "

" Well, by George ! " he cried, rising
and offering his hand with frank delight,
and introducing me in a single comprehensive wave to his wife and daughters.   " Yes,
sir," he went on, " and I wish I had an
Oboid here right now—up in the basement
of that stone boarding-house on the knoll
there—just for the sake of heating up, and
shutting down the valves, and blowing the
whole damned thing sky - high.   That
would suit me, sir, right down to the
ground."

" We're strangers here, sir," he explained
in answer to my question : " we'd seen a
good deal of the Dutch at home—I mean
our home—and we thought we'd like to
take a look at 'em in the place they come

from. Well, sir, we've had our look, and
we're satisfied. We don't want any more
on our plate, thank you. One helping is
an elegant sufficiency. Do you know the
trick they played on us? Why, I took a
team of horses yesterday from a place they
called Ibsenburg or Ilsenburg, or some such
name, and had it explained to my driver
that he was to take us up to the top of the
Brocken, there, and stop all night, and
fetch us back this morning. When we got
up as far as Shierke, there, it was getting
pretty dark, and the women - folks were
nervous, and so we laid up for the night.
There didn't seem anything for the driver
to do but set around in the kitchen and
drink beer, and he needed money for that,
and so I gave him some loose silver, and
told him to make himself at home. We
got the words out of a dictionary for that
—*machen sie selbst zu Heim* we figured
'em out to be—and I spoke them at him
slowly and distinctly, so that he had no
earthly excuse for not understanding. But,
would you believe it, sir, the miserable cuss

just up and skipped out, horses, rig and all, while we were getting supper! And here we were this morning, landed high and dry. No conveyance, nobody to comprehend a word of English, no nothing. We haven't seen the top of their darned mountain even."

"What I'm more concerned about, I tell Wilbur," put in the lady, "is seeing the bottom of .it. If they had only sense enough to make valises and bonnet-boxes ball-shaped, we could have rolled 'em down hill."

"There'll be no trouble about all that," I assured them, and we talked for a little about the simple enough process of getting their luggage carried down to the village, and of finding a vehicle there. I, indeed, agreed to make one of their party on quitting the Harz, that very afternoon.

"And now tell me about the Grundys," I urged, when these more pressing matters were out of the way. "I got a wire to-day saying—hinting that they are in luck's way again."

K

"Is that so ?" exclaimed the American, at once surprised and pleased. "I'm glad to hear it. I can't guess what it might be in. Grundy's got so many irons in the fire—some white hot, some lukewarm, some frosted straight through—you never can tell. The funny thing is—he can't tell himself. Why, sir, those men of yours in the City of London, they don't know any more about business than a babe unborn. If they were in New York they'd have their eye-teeth skinned out of their heads in the shake of a lamb's tail. Why, we've been milking them dry for a dozen years back. And yet, you know, somehow—— "

"Somehow— ?" I echoed, encouragingly.

"Well, sir, somehow—that's the odd thing about it—they don't stay milked."

*Disclosing the Educational Influence
exerted by the Essex Coast, and other
Matters, including Reasons for Joy*

"Sit down here by the fire—no, in the
easy chair," said Ermyntrude, with a note
of solicitude in her kindly voice. "Mamma
won't be home for half an hour yet, and I
want a nice, quiet, serious talk with you.
Oh, it's going to be extremely serious, and
you must begin by playing that you are at
least one hundred and fifty years old."

"That won't be so difficult," I replied,
not without the implication of injury. "It
will only be adding a few decades to the
venerableness that I seem always to possess
in your eyes."

"Oh!" said Ermie, and looked at me
inquiringly for a moment. Then she
seated herself, and gazed with much steadi-

ness into the fire. I waited for the nice,
serious talk to begin—and waited a long
time.

" Well, my dear child," I broke in upon
the silence at last, " I hoped to have been
the very first to come and tell your mother
how deeply glad I was to see you all back
again in Fernbank. But that wretched
rheumatism of mine—*at my age*, you
know——"

I was watching narrowly for even the
faintest sign of deprecation. She did not
stir an eyelash.

" Yes," she suddenly began, still intently
gazing into the fire ; "papa has got his
money all back, and more. That is, it
isn't the same money, but somebody else's
—I'm sure I don't know whose. Sometimes I feel sorry for those other people,
whoever they are, who have had to give it
up to us. Then, other times, I am so glad
simply to be in again where it's warm that
I don't care."

" The firelight suits your face, Ermie," I
said, noting with the pleasure appropriate

to my position as the oldest friend of the
family, how sweetly the soft radiance played
upward upon the fair young rounded throat
and chin, and tipped the little nostrils with
rosy light.

" Fortunately," she went on, as if I had
not spoken, "some Americans took the
house furnished in September for three
months—I think, poor souls, that they
believed it was the London season—and so
we never had to break up, and we were
able to get back again in time for Uncle
Dudley to plant all his bulbs. They seem
to have been very quiet people. Mamma
had a kind of notion that they would
practise with bucking horses on the tennis-
lawn, and shoot at bottles and clay pigeons
here in the drawing-room. The only thing
we could find that they did was to paste
thick paper over the ventilator in the
dining-room. And yet a policeman told
our man that they slept with their bed-
room windows open all night. Curious,
isn't it ? "

" I like to have one of these ' nice,

quiet, serious talks' with you, Ermie," I said.

Even at this she did not lift her eyes from the grate. " Oh, don't be impatient —it will be serious enough," she warned me. " They say, you know, that drowning people see, in a single instant of time, whole years of events, whole books full of things. Well, I've been under water for six months, and—and—I've noticed a good deal."

" Ah ! is there a submarine observation station at Clacton-on-Sea ? Now you speak of it, I *have* heard of queer fish being studied there."

" None queerer than we, my dear friend, you may be sure. Mamma was right in choosing the place. We never once saw a soul we knew. Of course, it is the dullest and commonest thing on earth—but it exactly fitted us during that awful period. We were going at first to Cromer, but mamma learned that that was the chosen resort of dissolute theatrical people—it seems there has been a poem written in

which it is called "Poppyland," which
mamma saw at once must be a cover for
opium-eating and all sorts of dissipation.
So we went to Clacton instead.   But what
I was going to say is this—I did a great
deal of thinking all through those six
months.   I don't say that I am any wiser
than I was, because, for that matter, I am
very much less sure about things than I
was before.   But I was simply a blank
contented fool then.   Now it's different to
the extent that I've stirred up all sorts of
questions and problems buzzing and bark-
ing about me, and I don't know the
answers to them, and I can't get clear of
them, and they're driving me out of my
head—and there you are.   That's what I
wanted to talk with you about."

I shifted my feet on the fender, and
nodded with as sensible an expression as I
could muster.

"That's why I said you must pretend to
yourself that you are very old—quite a
fatherly person, capable of giving a girl
advice—sympathetic advice. · In the first

place—of course you know that the engage-
ment with that Hon. Knobbeleigh Jones
has been off for ages.   Don't interrupt me !
It isn't worth speaking of except for one
point.   His father, Lord Skillyduff, was the
principal rogue in the combination which
plundered papa of his money.   Having got
the Grundy money they had no use for the
Grundy girl.   Now, he justified his ras-
cality by pleading that he had to make
provision for *his* daughters, and everybody
said he was a good father.   Papa goes in
again through some other opening, and
after a long fight brings out a fresh fortune,
which he has taken away from somebody
else—and I heard him tell mamma that he
was doing it for the sake of *his* daughters.
People will say *he* is a good father—I
know *I* do."

"None better in this world," I assented
cordially.

",Well, don't you see," Ermyntrude went
on, ",that puts daughters in the light of a
doubtful blessing.   Papa's whole worry and
struggle was for us—for *me*.   I was the

load on his back. I don't like to be a
load. While we were prosperous, there
was only one way for me to get down—
that is by marriage. When we became
poor, there was another way — that I
should earn my own living. But this
papa wouldn't listen to. He quite swore
about it—vowed he would rather work his
fingers to the bone; rather do anything, no
matter what it was, or what people thought
of him for doing it, than that a daughter
of his should take care of herself. He
would look upon himself as disgraced, he
said. Those lodgings of ours at Clacton
weren't specially conducive to good temper,
I'm afraid; for I told him that the real
disgrace would be to keep me in idleness
to sell to some other Knobbeleigh Jones,
or to palm me off on some better sort of
young man who would bind himself to
work for me all his life, and then find that
I would have been dear at the price of a
fortnight's labour—and then mamma cried
—and papa, he swore more—and—and—"

I stirred the fire here, and then blushed

to rediscover that it was asbestos I was knocking about. "How stupid of me !" I exclaimed, and murmured something about having been a stranger to Fernbank so long.

Ermyntrude took no notice. "I made a pretence of going up to London on a visit," she continued, "and I spent five days looking about, making inquiries, trying to get some notion of how girls who supported themselves made a beginning. I talked a little with such few girls that I knew as were in town, and I cared to see —guardedly, of course. They had no idea —save in the way of the governess or music teacher. I'd cut my throat before I'd be either of those—forced to dress like ladies on the wages of a seamstress, and to smile under the insults of tradesmen's wives and their louts of children. An actress I might be, after I had starved a long time in learning my business—but before that mamma would have died of shame. Then there are typewriters, and lady journalists and telegraph clerks—I am surly enough

sometimes to do that last to perfection—but
they all have to have special talents or
knowledge.   As for saleswomen in the
shops—there are a dozen poor genteel
wretches standing outside ready to claw
each other's eyes out for every vacancy.   I
went over Euston Road way at noon, and I
watched the work-girls come out of the
factories and workshops, and they had such
sharp, knowing, bullying faces that I knew
I should be a helpless fool among them.
And watching them—and watching the
other girls on the street . . . in the
Strand and Piccadilly—I told you I was
going to talk seriously, my dear friend—it
all came to seem to me like a nightmare.   It
frightened me.   These were the girls whose
fathers had failed to provide for them—
that was absolutely all the difference
between them and me.   I had looked
lazily down at marriage as a chance of
escaping being bored here at Fernbank.
They were all looking fiercely up at
marriage as the one only chance of rescue
from weary toil, starvation wages, general

poverty and misery. In both cases the
idea was the same—to find some man, no
matter what kind of a man, if only he will
take it upon himself to provide something
different. You see what poor, dependent
things we really are ! Why should it be
so ? That's what I want to know."

"Oh, that's all you want to know, is it ?"
I remarked, after a little pause. "Well, I
think—I think you had better give me
notice of the question."

"I have tried to read what thinkers say
about it," she added ; "but they only confuse one the more. There is a Dr Wallace
whom the papers speak of as an authority,
and he has been writing a long article this
very week—or else it is an interview—and
he says that everything will be all right,
that all the nice women will marry all the
good men, and that the other kinds will
die off immediately, and everybody will be
oh, so happy—in a 'regenerated society.'
That is another thing I wanted to ask you
about. He speaks—they all speak—so
confidently about this 'regenerated society.'

Do you happen to know when it is to
be ? "

" The date has not been fixed, I believe,"
I replied.

The early winter twilight had darkened
the room, and the light from the grate
glowed ruddily upon the girl's face as she
bent forward, her chin upon her clasped
hands, looking into the fire.

" There is another date which remains
undetermined," I added, faltering not a
little at heart, but keeping my tongue
under fair control.   " I should like to
speak to you about it, if I may take off
my lamb's-wool wig and Santa Claus beard,
and appear before you once more as a contemporary citizen.   It is this, Ermie.   I
am not so very old, after all.   There is
only a shade over a dozen years between us
—say a baker's dozen.   My habits—my
personal qualities, tolerable and otherwise,
are more or less known to you.   I am
prosperous enough, so far as this world's
goods go.   But I am tired of living——"

I stopped short, and stared in turn
blankly at the mock coals.   A freezing

thought had just thrust itself into the
marrow of my brain. She would think
that I was saying all this because her
father had regained and augmented his
fortune. I strove in a numb, puzzled way
to retrace what I had just uttered—to see
if the words offered any chance of getting
away upon other ground—and could not
remember at all.

"Tired of living," I heard Ermyntrude
echo. I saw her nod her head compre-
hendingly in the firelight. She sighed.

"Yes, except upon conditions," I burst
forth. "I weary of living alone. There
hasn't been a time for years when I didn't
long to tell you this—and most of all at
Clacton, if I had known you were at
Clacton. You have admitted yourself that
nobody knew you were there." The
words came more easily now. "But
always before I shrank from speaking.
There was something about you too child-
like, too innocent, too—too——"

"Too silly," suggested Ermie, with an
affable effect of helping me out.

Then she unlocked her fingers, and, still looking into the fire, stretched out a hand backward to me. "All the same," she murmured, after a little, "it isn't an answer to my question, you know."

"But it is to mine!" I made glad response, "and in my question all the others are enwrapped—always have been, always will be. And, oh, darling one——"

"That is mamma in the hall," said Ermyntrude.

Describing Impressions of a Momentous Interview, loosely gathered by One who, although present, was not quite In it

MRS ALBERT has smiled upon my suit to be her son-in-law.

The smile did not, however, gush forth spontaneously at the outset. When the opportunity for imparting our great news came, we three were in the drawing-room, and Mrs Albert, who had just entered, had been allowed to discover me holding Ermyntrude's passive hand in mine. She cast a swift little glance over us both, and seemed not to like what she saw. I was conscious of the impression on the instant that Ermyntrude did not particularly like it either. An effect of profound isolation, absurd enough, but depressingly real,

suddenly encompassed me. I began talking something—the words coming out and
scattering quite on their own incoherent
account—and the gist of what they made
me say sounded in my ears as if it were
a determined enemy who was saying it.
Why should I be speaking of my age, and
the fact that I had held Ermie on my knee
as a child, and even of my rheumatism?
And did I actually allude to them? or
only hear the clamorous echoes of conscience
in my guilty soul, the while my tongue was
uttering other matters? I don't know,
and the fear that Ermie would admit that
she really hadn't been paying attention has
restrained me from asking her since.

But Mrs Albert was paying attention.
She held me with a cool and unblinking eye
during my clumsy monologue, and she continued this steady gaze for a time after I
had finished. She stirred the small and
shapely headgear of black velvet and bird's-
wing which she had worn in from the
street, just by the fraction of a forward
inch, to show that she understood what I

L

had been saying—and also very much which I had left unsaid.

"Hm—m !" the good lady remarked, at length. "I see !"

"Well, mamma, having seen," Ermyntrude turned languidly in her chair to observe, lifting the hand which still rested within mine into full and patent view, and then withdrawing it abruptly—"having seen, and been seen, there's really nothing more to do, is there ?"

"She is very young," said the mother, in a tentative musing manner which suggested the thought that I, on the other hand, was very much the other way.

Ermyntrude sniffed audibly, and rose to her feet. "I am three-and-twenty," she said, "and that is enough, thank you."

There was something in it all which I did not understand. The sensation of being out of place, as in the trying-on room of a dressmaker's, oppressed me. The sex were effecting sundry manœuvres and countermarchings peculiar to themselves— so much I could see by the way in which

the two were talking with their eyes—
but what it was all about was beyond me.
The mother finally inclined her head to
one side, and pursed together her lips.
Ermyntrude drew herself to her full stature,
threw up her chin for a moment like one
of Albert Moore's superb full - throated
goddesses, and then relaxed with that half-
cheerful sigh which we express in types
with "heigho!" It was at once apparent
to me that the situation had lightened—
but how or why I cannot profess to guess.
Uncle Dudley, to whom I subsequently
narrated what I had observed, abounded in
theories, but upon reflection they do not
impress, much less convince, me. Here is
in substance one of the several hypothetical
conversations which he sketched out as
having passed in that moment of pre-occu-
pied and surcharged silence :

MOTHER [*lowering brows*]. You may be sure that
at the very best it will be Bayswater.

DAUGHTER [*with quiver of nostrils*]. Better that
than hanging on for a Belgravia which never
comes.

MOTHER [*disclosing the tips of two teeth*].   It is a
chance of a title going for ever.

DAUGHTER [*curling lip*].   What chance is ever
likely *here?*

MOTHER [*lifting brows*].   He's as old as Methu-
saleh !"

DAUGHTER [*flashing eyes*].   That's my business !

MOTHER [*little trembling of the eyelashes*].   You
will never know how I have striven and struggled
for you !

DAUGHTER [*smoothing features*].   Merely the
innate maternal instinct, my dear, common to all
mammalia.

MOTHER [*beginning to tip head sidewise*].   It is
true that Tristram is docile, sheep-like, simple——

DAUGHTER [*lifting her chin*].   And old enough to
be enchained at my feet all his life.

MOTHER [*head much to one side*].   And he has
always been extremely cordial with *me*——

DAUGHTER [*chin high in air*].   And not another
girl in my set has had a proposal for *years.*

MOTHER [*brightening eye*].   We shall be in time
to buy everything at the January sales !

[MOTHER *smiles;* DAUGHTER *sighs relief. The
imaginations of both wander pleasantly off to visions
of sublimated Christmas shopping, in connection with
the trousseau and betrothal gifts.   General joy.*]

As I have said, this is Uncle Dudley's
idea, not mine. My own fancy prefers to
conjure up a tenderer dialogue, in which
the mother, all fond solicitude, bids the

maiden search well her heart, and answer
only its true appeal, and the sweet daughter,
timid, fluttering, half-frightened and wholly
glad, flashes back from the depths of her
soul the rapt assurance of her fate. But
Dudley was certainly right about the end-
ing, as the first words Mrs Albert uttered
go to show.

"Don't forget to remind me, then, about
presents for the Gregory children," she said
all at once, in a swift sidelong whisper at
Ermyntrude. Then she turned, and as I
gazed wistfully upon her face, it melted
sedately, gracefully, a little at a time, into
the smile I sought.

"My dear Tristram," she began, and her
voice took on a coo of genuine kindliness
and warmth as she went on, "of course
Albert and I have had other views—and
the dear girl is perfectly qualified to adorn
the most exalted and exclusive circles—if
I do say it myself—but—but her hap-
piness is our one desire, and if she feels
that it is getting—I *would* say, if you and
she are quite clear in your own minds—

and we both have the greatest confidence
in your practical common-sense, and your
honour—and we have all learned to be
fond of you—and—and I am really very
glad ! ”

“ Most of all things in the world, dear
lady, I hoped for this,” I had begun to say,
with fervour.   I stopped, upon the discovery that Mrs Albert was not listening,
but had turned and was conferring with
her daughter in half-audible asides.

“ Mercy, no ! ” the mother said. “ They’d
know in a minute that it had been a present
to us.   That old Mrs Gregory is a perfect
lynx for detecting such things.   I suppose
their boys are too big for tricycles, else your
father knows a dealer who——— ”

My own Ermie looked thoughtful.   “ It
won’t seem queer, you think, our bursting
in upon them with Christmas presents like
this—without provocation ? ” she asked.

“ My dear child, queer or not queer,”
said Mrs Albert, “ it is imperative.   You
know how much depends upon it—there
are plenty of others who would be equally

useful in various ways, but not like the *Gregorys*—and if there were there's no time now. If this could have happened, now, a fortnight ago, or even last week—— "

" Yes, but it didn't," replied Ermyntrude. " It only happened to-day." She turned to me, with a little laugh in her eyes. " Mamma complains that we 'delayed so long. We have interfered with the Christmas arrangements."

" If I had only known ! But—I claim to be treated as one of the family, you know —I couldn't quite grasp what you were saying about the Gregorys. I gather that our — our betrothal involves Christmas presents for them, but I confess I don't know why. Or oughtn't I to have asked, dear ? "

For answer Ermyntrude looked saucily into my face, twisted her dear nose into a pretty little mocking grimace, and ran out of the room. Mrs Albert vouchsafed no explanation, but talked of other matters— and there were enough to talk about.

It was not, indeed, till late in the evening, when Uncle Dudley and I were upon our last cigar, that I happened to recall the mystifying incident of the Gregorys.

" That's simplicity itself," said Uncle Dudley. The Gregorys own one of the tidiest country seats in Nottinghamshire— lovely old house, sylvan arbours, high wall, fascinating rural roads—in the very heart of county society, too—O, a most romantic and eligible place ! "

" Well, what of it ? What has that to do with Ermyntrude and me and Santa Claus ? "

" If you will read the *Morning Post* the day after your wedding, my dear, dull friend, you will learn that Colonel Gregory has placed at the disposal of a certain bridal couple for their honeymoon his ideal country residence. The paper will not state why, but I will tell you in confidence. It will be because the bride's mother is a resourceful and observant woman, who knows how to plant at Christmas that she may gather at Easter."

" I hate to have you always so beastly cynical, Dudley," I was emboldened to exclaim.

Uncle Dudley regarded me attentively for an instant. He took a thoughtful sip at his drink, and then began smiling at his glass. When he turned to me again, the smile had grown into a grin.

" You are belated, my boy," he said. " You ought to have married into the Grundys years ago. You were just born to be one of the family."

TURNBULL AND SPEARS, PRINTERS, EDINBURGH.

1896.

List of Books

IN

BELLES LETTRES

(*Including some Transfers*)

Published by John Lane

𝖳𝔥𝔢 𝔅𝔬𝔡𝔩𝔢𝔭 𝔥𝔢𝔞𝔡

VIGO STREET, LONDON, W.

N.B.—*The Authors and Publisher reserve the right of reprinting
any book in this list if a new edition is called for, except in cases
where a stipulation has been made to the contrary, and of printing
a separate edition of any of the books for America irrespective of the
numbers to which the English editions are limited. The numbers
mentioned do not include copies sent to the public libraries, nor those
sent for review.*
*Most of the books are published simultaneously in England and
America, and in many instances the names of the American
Publishers are appended.*

ADAMS (FRANCIS).
    ESSAYS IN MODERNITY. Crown 8vo. 5s. net. [*Shortly.*
      Chicago : Stone & Kimball.
    A CHILD OF THE AGE. (*See* KEYNOTES SERIES.)
ALDRICH (T. B.).
    LATER LYRICS. Sm. fcap. 8vo, 2s. 6d. net.
      Boston and New York : Houghton, Mifflin & Co.
ALLEN (GRANT).
    THE LOWER SLOPES : A Volume of Verse. With Title-
      page and Cover Design by J. ILLINGWORTH KAY.
      600 copies. Crown 8vo. 5s. net.
      Chicago : Stone & Kimball.
    THE WOMAN WHO DID. (*See* KEYNOTES SERIES.)
    THE BRITISH BARBARIANS. (*See* KEYNOTES SERIES.)
BAILEY (JOHN C).
    AN ANTHOLOGY OF ENGLISH ELEGIES. [*In preparation.*

BEARDSLEY (AUBREY).

THE STORY OF VENUS AND TANNHÄUSER, in which is set forth an exact account of the Manner of State held by Madam Venus, Goddess and Meretrix, under the famous Hörselberg, and containing the adventures of Tannhäuser in that place, his repentance, his journeying to Rome, and return to the loving mountain. By AUBREY BEARDSLEY. With 20 full-page Illustrations, numerous ornaments, and a cover from the same hand. Sq. 16mo. 10s. 6d. net. [*In preparation.*

BEECHING (REV. H. C.).

IN A GARDEN : Poems. With Title-page designed by ROGER FRY. Crown 8vo. 5s. net.
New York : Macmillan & Co.

BENSON (ARTHUR CHRISTOPHER).

LYRICS. Fcap. 8vo, buckram. 5s. net.
New York : Macmillan & Co.

BRIDGES (ROBERT).

SUPPRESSED CHAPTERS AND OTHER BOOKISHNESS. Crown 8vo. 3s. 6d. net.
New York : Charles Scribner's Sons.

BROTHERTON (MARY).

ROSEMARY FOR REMEMBRANCE. With Title-page and Cover Design by WALTER WEST. Fcap. 8vo. 3s. 6d. net.

BUCHAN (JOHN).

MUSA PISCATRIX. [*In preparation.*

CASE (ROBERT).

AN ANTHOLOGY OF ENGLISH EPITHALAMIES.
[*In preparation.*

CRAIG (R. MANIFOLD).

THE SACRIFICE OF FOOLS : A Novel. Crown 8vo. 4s. 6d. net. [*In preparation.*

CRANE (WALTER).

TOY BOOKS. Re-issue. Each with new Cover Design and end papers. 9d. net.
The group of three bound in one volume, with a decorative cloth cover, end papers, and a newly written and designed title-page and preface. 3s. 6d. net.
I. THIS LITTLE PIG.
II. THE FAIRY SHIP.
III. KING LUCKIEBOY'S PARTY.
Chicago : Stone & Kimball.

DALMON (C. W.).

SONG FAVOURS. With a Title-page designed by J. P.
DONNE. Sq. 16mo. 3s. 6d. net.
Chicago: Way & Williams.

DAVIDSON (JOHN).

PLAYS: An Unhistorical Pastoral; A Romantic Farce;
Bruce, a Chronicle Play; Smith, a Tragic Farce;
Scaramouch in Naxos, a Pantomime, with a Frontis-
piece and Cover Design by AUBREY BEARDSLEY.
Printed at the Ballantyne Press. 500 copies. Small
4to. 7s. 6d. net.
Chicago: Stone & Kimball.

FLEET STREET ECLOGUES. Fcap. 8vo, buckram. 4s. 6d.
net. [*Third Edition*.
FLEET STREET ECLOGUES. 2nd Series. Fcap. 8vo,
buckram. 4s. 6d. net.

A RANDOM ITINERARY AND A BALLAD. With a Frontispiece and Title-page by LAURENCE HOUSMAN.
600 copies. Fcap. 8vo, Irish Linen. 5s. net.
Boston: Copeland & Day.

BALLADS AND SONGS. With a Title-page and Cover
Design by WALTER WEST. Fourth Edition. Fcap.
8vo, buckram. 5s. net.
Boston: Copeland & Day.

DE TABLEY (LORD).

POEMS, DRAMATIC AND LYRICAL. By JOHN LEICESTER
WARREN (Lord De Tabley). Illustrations and Cover
Design by C. S. RICKETTS. Third Edition. Crown
8vo. 7s. 6d. net.
New York: Macmillan & Co.

POEMS, DRAMATIC AND LYRICAL. Second Series, uniform in binding with the former volume. Crown 8vo.
5s. net.
New York: Macmillan & Co.

EGERTON (GEORGE).

KEYNOTES. (*See* KEYNOTES SERIES.)
DISCORDS. (*See* KEYNOTES SERIES.)
YOUNG OFEG'S DITTIES. A translation from the Swedish
of OLA HANSSON. With Title-page and Cover Design
by AUBREY BEARDSLEY. Crown 8vo. 3s. 6d. net.
Boston: Roberts Bros.

FARR (FLORENCE).

THE DANCING FAUN. (*See* KEYNOTES SERIES.

FLEMING (GEORGE).
    FOR PLAIN WOMEN ONLY. (*See* MAYFAIR SET.)

FLETCHER (J. S.).
    THE WONDERFUL WAPENTAKE. By 'A SON OF THE
        SOIL.' With 18 full-page Illustrations by J. A.
        SYMINGTON. Crown 8vo. 5s. 6d. net.
        Chicago: A. C. McClurg & Co.

FREDERIC (HAROLD).
    MRS ALBERT GRUNDY. (*See* MAYFAIR SET.)

GALE (NORMAN).
    ORCHARD SONGS. With Title-page and Cover Design
        by J. ILLINGWORTH KAY. Fcap 8vo, Irish Linen.
        5s. net.
        Also a Special Edition limited in number on hand-made paper
        bound in English vellum. £1, 1s. net.
        New York: G. P. Putnam's Sons.

GARNETT (RICHARD).
    POEMS. With Title-page by J. ILLINGWORTH KAY.
        350 copies. Crown 8vo. 5s. net.
        Boston: Copeland & Day.
    DANTE, PETRARCH, CAMOENS, cxxiv Sonnets rendered
        in English. Crown 8vo. 5s. net. [*In preparation.*

GEARY (SIR NEVILL, BART.).
    A LAWYER'S WIFE: A Novel. Crown 8vo. 4s. 6d.
        net. [*In preparation.*

GIBSON (CHARLES DANA).
    PICTURES: Nearly One Hundred Large Cartoons. Ob-
        long Folio. 15s. net.
        New York: R. H. Russell & Son.

GOSSE (EDMUND).
    THE LETTERS OF THOMAS LOVELL BEDDOES. Now
        first edited. Pott 8vo. 5s. net.
        Also 25 copies large paper. 12s. 6d. net.
        New York: Macmillan & Co.

GRAHAME (KENNETH).
    PAGAN PAPERS: A Volume of Essays. With Title-
        page by AUBREY BEARDSLEY. Fcap. 8vo. 5s. net.
        Chicago: Stone & Kimball.
                [*Out of print at present.*
    THE GOLDEN AGE. Crown 8vo. Second Edition.
        3s. 6d. net.
        Chicago: Stone & Kimball.

GREENE (G. A.).
ITALIAN LYRISTS OF TO-DAY. Translations in the
original metres from about thirty-five living Italian
poets, with bibliographical and biographical notes.
Crown 8vo. 5s. net.
New York : Macmillan & Co.
GREENWOOD (FREDERICK).
IMAGINATION IN DREAMS. Crown 8vo. 5s. net.
New York : Macmillan & Co.
HAKE (T. GORDON).
A SELECTION FROM HIS POEMS. Edited by Mrs
MEYNELL. With a Portrait after D. G. ROSSETTI,
and a Cover Design by GLEESON WHITE. Crown
8vo. 5s. net.
Chicago : Stone and Kimball.
HANSSON (LAURA MARHOLM).
MODERN WOMEN : Six Psychological Sketches. [Sophia
Kovalevsky, George Egerton, Eleanora Duse, Amalie
Skram, Marie Bashkirtseff, A. Edgren Leffler.] Trans-
lated from the German by HERMIONE RAMSDEN.
Crown 8vo. 3s. 6d. net.
HANSSON (OLA). See EGERTON.
HARLAND (HENRY).
GREY ROSES. (See KEYNOTES SERIES.)
HAYES (ALFRED).
THE VALE OF ARDEN AND OTHER POEMS. With a
Title-page and a Cover designed by E. H. NEW.
Fcap. 8vo. 3s. 6d. net.
Also 25 copies large paper. 15s. net.
HAZLITT (WILLIAM).
LIBER AMORIS, OR THE NEW PYGMALION. A New
Edition from the Original MS. With Letters and a
Diary never before printed. Portrait after BEWICK,
and Facsimiles, and a lengthy Introduction by
RICHARD LE GALLIENNE. 4to, buckram. 21s. net.
HEINEMANN (WILLIAM).
THE FIRST STEP. A Dramatic Moment. Small 4to.
3s. 6d. net.
HOPPER (NORA).
BALLADS IN PROSE. With a Title-page and Cover by
WALTER WEST. Sq. 16mo. 5s. net.
Boston : Roberts Bros.
UNDER QUICKEN BOUGHS. With Title-page designed by
PATTEN WILSON. Cr. 8vo. 5s. net.

HOUSMAN (CLEMENCE).

THE WERE WOLF. With six Full-page Illustrations, Title-page and Cover Design, by LAURENCE HOUS-MAN. Sq. 16mo. 3s. 6d. net.

HOUSMAN (LAURENCE).

GREEN ARRAS: Poems. With Illustrations by the Author. Crown 8vo. 5s. net. [*In preparation.*

IRVING (LAURENCE).

GODEFROI AND YOLANDE: A Play. With three Illus-' trations by AUBREY BEARDSLEY. Sm. 4to. 5s. net.
[*In preparation.*

JAMES (W. P.).

ROMANTIC PROFESSIONS: A Volume of Essays. With Title - page designed by J. ILLINGWORTH KAY. Crown 8vo. 5s. net.
New York: Macmillan & Co.

JOHNSON (LIONEL).

THE ART OF THOMAS HARDY: Six Essays. With Etched Portrait by WM. STRANG, and Bibliography by JOHN LANE. Second Edition. Crown 8vo. 5s. 6d. net.

Also 150 copies, large paper, with proofs of the portrait. £1, 1s. net.

New York: Dodd, Mead & Co.

JOHNSON (PAULINE).

WHITE WAMPUM: Poems. With a Title-page and Cover Design by E. H. NEW. Crown 8vo. 5s. net.
Boston: Lamson, Wolffe & Co.

JOHNSTONE (C. E.).

BALLADS OF BOY AND BEAK. With a Title-page designed by F. H. TOWNSEND. Sq. 32mo. 2s. net.

KEYNOTES SERIES.

Each volume with specially designed Title-page by AUBREY BEARDSLEY. Crown 8vo, cloth. 3s. 6d. net.

Vol. I. KEYNOTES. By GEORGE EGERTON.
[*Seventh edition now ready.*
Vol. II. THE DANCING FAUN. By FLORENCE FARR.
Vol. III. POOR FOLK. Translated from the Russian of F. Dostoievsky by LENA MILMAN. With a Preface by GEORGE MOORE.
Vol. IV. A CHILD OF THE AGE. By FRANCIS ADAMS.

KEYNOTES SERIES—*continued*.
Vol. V. THE GREAT GOD PAN AND THE INMOST
LIGHT. By ARTHUR MACHEN.
[*Second edition now ready.*
Vol. VI. DISCORDS. By GEORGE EGERTON.
[*Fourth edition now ready.*
Vol. VII. PRINCE ZALESKI. By M. P. SHIEL.
Vol. VIII. THE WOMAN WHO DID. By GRANT ALLEN.
[*Nineteenth edition now ready.*
Vol. IX. WOMEN'S TRAGEDIES. By H. D. LOWRY.
Vol. X. GREY ROSES. By HENRY HARLAND.
Vol. XI. AT THE FIRST CORNER AND OTHER STORIES.
By H. B. MARRIOTT WATSON.
Vol. XII. MONOCHROMES. By ELLA D'ARCY.
Vol. XIII. AT THE RELTON ARMS. By EVELYN SHARP.
Vol. XIV. THE GIRL FROM THE FARM. By GERTRUDE
DIX. [*Second edition now ready.*
Vol. XV. THE MIRROR OF MUSIC. By STANLEY V.
MAKOWER.
Vol. XVI. YELLOW AND WHITE. By W. CARLTON
DAWE.
Vol. XVII. THE MOUNTAIN LOVERS. By FIONA
MACLEOD.
Vol. XVIII. THE WOMAN WHO DIDN'T. By VICTORIA
CROSSE. [*Second edition now ready.*
Vol. XIX. THE THREE IMPOSTORS. By ARTHUR
MACHEN.
Vol. XX. NOBODY'S FAULT. By NETTA SYRETT.
Vol. XXI. THE BRITISH BARBARIANS. By GRANT ALLEN.
The following are in rapid preparation.
Vol. XXII. IN HOMESPUN. By E. NESBIT.
Vol. XXIII. PLATONIC AFFECTIONS. By JOHN SMITH.
Vol. XXIV. NETS FOR THE WIND. By UNA TAYLOR.
Vol. XXV. WHERE THE ATLANTIC MEETS THE LAND.
By CALDWELL LIPSETT.
Boston : Roberts Bros.

KING (MAUDE EGERTON).
ROUND ABOUT A BRIGHTON COACH OFFICE. With 30
Illustrations by LUCY KEMP WELCH. Cr. 8vo.
5s. net.

LANDER (HARRY).
WEIGHED IN THE BALANCE ; A Novel. Crown 8vo.
4s. 6d. net. [*In preparation.*

LANG (ANDREW). *See* STODDART.

LEATHER (R. K.).
VERSES. 250 copies. Fcap. 8vo. 3s. net.
Transferred by the Author to the present Publisher.

LE GALLIENNE (RICHARD).
PROSE FANCIES. With Portrait of the Author by
WILSON STEER. Fourth Edition. Crown 8vo.
Purple cloth. 5s. net.
Also a limited large paper edition. 12s. 6d. net.
New York : G. P. Putnam's Sons.

THE BOOK BILLS OF NARCISSUS, An Account rendered
by RICHARD LE GALLIENNE. Third Edition. With
a Frontispiece. Crown 8vo. Purple cloth. 3s. 6d. net.
Also 50 copies on large paper. 8vo. 10s. 6d. net.
New York : G. P. Putman's Sons.

ROBERT LOUIS STEVENSON, AN ELEGY, AND OTHER
POEMS, MAINLY PERSONAL. With Etched Title-page
by D. Y. CAMERON. Cr. 8vo. Purple cloth. 4s. 6d. net.
Also 75 copies on large paper. 8vo. 12s. 6d. net.
Boston : Copeland & Day.

ENGLISH POEMS. Fourth Edition, revised. Crown 8vo.
Purple cloth. 4s. 6d. net.
Boston : Copeland & Day.

RETROSPECTIVE REVIEWS, A LITERARY LOG, 1891-1895.
2 vols. crown 8vo. Purple cloth. 9s. net.
[*In preparation.*
New York : Dodd, Mead & Co.

GEORGE MEREDITH : Some Characteristics. With a Bibliography (much enlarged) by JOHN LANE, Portrait, etc.
Fourth Edition. Cr. 8vo. Purple cloth. 5s. 6d. net.

THE RELIGION OF A LITERARY MAN. 5th thousand.
Crown 8vo. Purple cloth. 3s. 6d. net.
Also a special rubricated edition on hand-made paper. 8vo
10s. 6d. net.
New York : G. P. Putnam's Sons.
See also HAZLITT.

LIPSETT (CALDWELL).
WHERE THE ATLANTIC MEETS THE LAND. (*See* KEY-
NOTES SERIES.)

LOWRY (H. D.).
WOMEN'S TRAGEDIES. (*See* KEYNOTES SERIES.)

LUCAS (WINIFRED).

A VOLUME OF POEMS.   Fcap. 8vo.   4s. 6d. net.
                                              [*In preparation.*

LYNCH (HANNAH).

THE GREAT GALEOTO AND FOLLY OR SAINTLINESS. Two
    Plays, from the Spanish of JOSÉ ECHEGARAY, with an
    Introduction. Small 4to.   5s. 6d. net.
    Boston : Lamson, Wolffe & Co.

MACHEN (ARTHUR).

THE GREAT GOD PAN.   (*See* KEYNOTES SERIES.)
THE THREE IMPOSTORS.   (*See* KEYNOTES SERIES.)

MACLEOD (FIONA).

THE MOUNTAIN LOVERS.   (*See* KEYNOTES SERIES.)

MAKOWER (STANLEY V.).

THE MIRROR OF MUSIC.   (*See* KEYNOTES SERIES.)

MARZIALS (THEO.).

THE GALLERY OF PIGEONS AND OTHER POEMS. Post
    8vo. 4s. 6d. net.   [*Very few remain.*
    Transferred by the Author to the present Publisher.

MATHEW (FRANK).

THE WOOD OF THE BRAMBLES : A Novel. With Title-
    page and Cover Design by PATTEN WILSON. Crown
    8vo. 4s. 6d. net.

THE MAYFAIR SET.

Each volume fcap. 8vo. 3s. 6d. net.

Vol. I. THE AUTOBIOGRAPHY OF A BOY : Passages
    selected by his Friend, G. S. STREET. With a Title-
    page designed by C. W. FURSE.
                                  [*Fifth Edition now ready.*

Vol. II. THE JONESES AND THE ASTERISKS : a Story in
    Monologue. By GERALD CAMPBELL. With Title-
    page and six Illustrations by F. H. TOWNSEND.
                                  [*Second Edition now ready.*

Vol. III. SELECT CONVERSATIONS WITH AN UNCLE NOW
    EXTINCT. By H. G. WELLS. With Title-page by
    F. H. TOWNSEND.

Vol. IV. FOR PLAIN WOMEN ONLY. By GEORGE
    FLEMING.

THE MAYFAIR SET—*continued.*

Vol. v. THE FEASTS OF AUTOLYCUS: The Diary oi a
Greedy Woman. Edited by ELIZABETH ROBINS
PENNELL. With Title-page by PATTEN WILSON.

Vol. vi. MRS ALBERT GRUNDY: Observations in Philistia.
By HAROLD FREDERIC. With Title-page by PATTEN
WILSON.

New York : The Merriam Company.

MEREDITH (GEORGE).

THE FIRST PUBLISHED PORTRAIT OF THIS AUTHOR,
engraved on the wood by W. BISCOMBE GARDNER,
after the painting by G. F. WATTS. Proof copies on
Japanese vellum, signed by painter and engraver.
£1, 1s. net.

MEYNELL (MRS), (ALICE C. THOMPSON).

POEMS. Fcap. 8vo. 3s. 6d. net. [*Third Edition.*
A few of the 50 large paper copies (First Edition) remain, 12s. 6d. net.

THE RHYTHM OF LIFE AND OTHER ESSAYS. Fcap.
8vo. 3s. 6d. net. [*Third Edition.*
A few of the 50 large paper copies (First Edition) remain, 12s. 6d. net.

See also HAKE.

MILLER (JOAQUIN).

THE BUILDING OF THE CITY BEAUTIFUL. Fcap. 8vo.
With a Decorated Cover. 5s. net.
Chicago : Stone & Kimball.

MILMAN (LENA).

DOSTOIEVSKY'S POOR FOLK. (*See* KEYNOTES SERIES.)

MONKHOUSE (ALLAN).

BOOKS AND PLAYS : A Volume of Essays on Meredith,
Borrow, Ibsen, and others. 400 copies. Crown 8vo.
5s. net.
Philadelphia : J. B. Lippincott Co.

MOORE (GEORGE).

See KEYNOTES SERIES, Vol. III.

NESBIT (E.).

A POMANDER OF VERSE. With a Title-page and Cover
designed by LAURENCE HOUSMAN. Crown 8vo.
5s. net.
Chicago: A. C. McClurg & Co.

IN HOMESPUN. (*See* KEYNOTES SERIES.)

NETTLESHIP (J. T.).

ROBERT BROWNING : Essays and Thoughts. Third Edition. With a Portrait. Crown 8vo. 5s. 6d. net. New York : Chas. Scribner's Sons.

NOBLE (JAS. ASHCROFT).

THE SONNET IN ENGLAND AND OTHER ESSAYS. Title-page and Cover Design by AUSTIN YOUNG. 600 copies. Crown 8vo. 5s. net.
Also 50 copies large paper. 12s. 6d. net.

O'SHAUGHNESSY (ARTHUR).

HIS LIFE AND HIS WORK. With Selections from his Poems. By LOUISE CHANDLER MOULTON. Portrait and Cover Design. Fcap. 8vo. 5s. net. Chicago : Stone & Kimball.

OXFORD CHARACTERS.

A series of lithographed portraits by WILL ROTHENSTEIN, with text by F. YORK POWELL and others. To be issued monthly in term. Each number will contain two portraits. Parts I. to VII. ready. 200 sets only, folio, wrapper, 5s. net per part ; 25 special large paper sets containing proof impressions of the portraits signed by the artist, 10s. 6d. net per part.

PENNELL (ELIZABETH ROBINS).

THE FEASTS OF AUTOLYCUS. (*See* MAYFAIR SET.)

PETERS (WM. THEODORE).

POSIES OUT OF RINGS. Sq. 16mo. 2s. net.
[In preparation.

PIERROT'S LIBRARY.

Each volume with Title-page, Cover Design, and End-papers designed by AUBREY BEARDSLEY. Sq. 16mo. 2s. net.

Vol. I. PIERROT. By H. DE VERE STACPOOLE.
The following are in preparation.
Vol. II. MY LITTLE LADY ANNE. By Mrs EGERTON CASTLE.
Vol. III. DEATH, THE KNIGHT AND THE LADY. By H. DE VERE STACPOOLE.
Vol. IV. SIMPLICITY. By A. T. G. PRICE.
Philadelphia : Henry Altemus.

PLARR (VICTOR).

IN THE DORIAN MOOD : Poems. With a Title-page by PATTEN WILSON. Crown 8vo. 5s. net.
[In preparation.

PRICE (A. T. G.).
 SIMPLICITY. (*See* PIERROT'S LIBRARY.)

RADFORD (DOLLIE).
 SONGS AND OTHER VERSES. With Title-page designed
  by PATTEN WILSON. Fcap. 8vo. 4s. 6d. net.
   Philadelphia : J. B. Lippincott Co.

RAMSDEN (HERMIONE).
 See HANSSON.

RHYS (ERNEST).
 A LONDON ROSE AND OTHER RHYMES. With Title-page
  designed by SELWYN IMAGE. 350 copies. Crown
  8vo. 5s. net.
   New York : Dodd, Mead & Co.

RICKETTS (C. S.) AND C. H. SHANNON.
 HERO AND LEANDER. By CHRISTOPHER MARLOWE
  and GEORGE CHAPMAN. With Borders, Initials, and
  Illustrations designed and engraved on the wood by
  C. S. RICKETTS and C. H. SHANNON. Bound in
  English vellum and gold. 200 copies only. 35s. net.
   Boston : Copeland & Day.

ROBERTSON (JOHN M.).
 ESSAYS TOWARDS A CRITICAL METHOD. (New Series.)
  Crown 8vo. 5s. net.   [*In preparation.*

ROBINSON (C. NEWTON).
 THE VIOL OF LOVE. With Ornaments and Cover Design
  by LAURENCE HOUSMAN. Crown 8vo. 5s. net.
   Boston : Lamson, Wolffe & Co.

ST. CYRES (LORD).
 THE LITTLE FLOWERS OF ST. FRANCIS : A new ren-
  dering into English of the Fioretti di San Francesco.
  Crown 8vo. 5s. net.   [*In preparation.*

SHARP (EVELYN).
 AT THE RELTON ARMS. (*See* KEYNOTES SERIES.)

SHIEL (M. P.).
 PRINCE ZALESKI. (*See* KEYNOTES SERIES.)

SMITH (JOHN).
 PLATONIC AFFECTIONS. (*See* KEYNOTES SERIES.)

STACPOOLE (H. DE VERE).
 PIERROT. (*See* PIERROT'S LIBRARY.)
 DEATH, THE KNIGHT AND THE LADY. (*See* PIERROT'S
  LIBRARY.)

STEVENSON (ROBERT LOUIS).
PRINCE OTTO. A rendering in French by EGERTON
CASTLE. Crown 8vo. 5s. net. [*In preparation.*
Also 100 copies on large paper, uniform in size with the Edinburgh
Edition of the Works.
A CHILD'S GARDEN OF VERSES. With nearly 100
Illustrations by CHARLES ROBINSON. Second Edition.
Crown 8vo. 5s. net.
STODDART (THOS. TOD).
THE DEATH WAKE. With an Introduction by ANDREW
LANG. Fcap. 8vo. 5s. net.
Chicago : Way & Williams.
STREET (G. S.).
MINIATURES AND MOODS. Fcap. 8vo. 3s. net.
Transferred by the Author to the present Publisher.
THE AUTOBIOGRAPHY OF A BOY. (*See* MAYFAIR SET.)
New York : The Merriam Co.
QUALES EGO ; a few remarks, in particular and at large.
Fcap. 8vo. 3s. 6d. net.
New York : The Merriam Co.
SWETTENHAM (F. A.).
MALAY SKETCHES. With Title-page and Cover Design
by PATTEN WILSON. Second Edition. Crown 8vo.
5s. net.
New York : Macmillan & Co.
SYRETT (NETTA).
NOBODY'S FAULT. (*See* KEYNOTES SERIES.)
TABB (JOHN B.).
POEMS. Sq. 32mo. 4s. 6d. net.
Boston : Copeland & Day.
TAYLOR (UNA).
NETS FOR THE WIND. (*See* KEYNOTES SERIES.)
TENNYSON (FREDERICK).
POEMS OF THE DAY AND YEAR. With a Title-page by
PATTEN WILSON. Crown 8vo. 5s. net.
Chicago : Stone & Kimball.
THIMM (C. A.).
A COMPLETE BIBLIOGRAPHY OF THE ART OF FENCE,
DUELLING, ETC. With Illustrations. [*In preparation.*
THOMPSON (FRANCIS).
POEMS. With Frontispiece, Title-page, and Cover Design
by LAURENCE HOUSMAN. Fourth Edition. Pott
4to. 5s. net.
Boston : Copeland & Day.

THOMPSON (FRANCIS)—*continued.*
> SISTER SONGS: An Offering to Two Sisters. With Frontis-
> piece, Title-page, and Cover Design by LAURENCE
> HOUSMAN. Pott 4to. 5s. net.
> > Boston: Copeland & Day.

THOREAU (HENRY DAVID).
> POEMS OF NATURE. Selected and edited by HENRY S.
> SALT and FRANK B. SANBORN, with a Title-page
> designed by PATTEN WILSON. Fcap. 8vo. 4s. 6d.
> net.
> > Boston and New York: Houghton, Mifflin & Co.

TRAILL (H. D.).
> THE BARBAROUS BRITISHERS: A Tip-top Novel. With
> Title and Cover Design by AUBREY BEARDSLEY.
> Crown 8vo. Wrapper, 1s. net.

TYNAN HINKSON (KATHARINE).
> CUCKOO SONGS. With Title-page and Cover Design by
> LAURENCE HOUSMAN. Fcap. 8vo. 5s. net.
> > Boston: Copeland & Day.
> MIRACLE PLAYS: OUR LORD'S COMING AND CHILDHOOD.
> With Six Illustrations, Title-page, and Cover Design
> by PATTEN WILSON. Fcap. 8vo. 4s. 6d. net.
> > Chicago: Stone & Kimball.

WATSON (ROSAMUND MARRIOTT).
> VESPERTILIA AND OTHER POEMS. With a Title-page
> designed by R. ANNING BELL. Fcap. 8vo. 4s. 6d.
> net.
> A SUMMER NIGHT AND OTHER POEMS. New edition,
> with a decorative Title-page. Fcap. 8vo. 3s. net.
> > Chicago: Way & Williams.

WATSON (H. B. MARRIOTT).
> AT THE FIRST CORNER. (*See* KEYNOTES SERIES.)
> GALLOPING DICK. With Title-page and Cover Design
> by PATTEN WILSON. Crown 8vo. 4s. 6d. net.
> > Chicago: Stone & Kimball.

WATSON (WILLIAM).
> THE FATHER OF THE FOREST, AND OTHER POEMS.
> With New Photogravure Portrait of the Author.
> Fifth Thousand. Fcap. 8vo. 3s. 6d. net.
> > 75 copies, large paper, 10s. 6d. net.
> > Chicago: Stone & Kimball.
> ODES AND OTHER POEMS. Fourth Edition. Fcap. 8vo,
> buckram. 4s. 6d. net.
> > New York: Macmillan & Co.

WATSON (WILLIAM)—*continued.*
THE ELOPING ANGELS : A Caprice. Second Edition.
Square 16mo, buckram. 3s. 6d. net.
New York : Macmillan & Co.
EXCURSIONS IN CRITICISM : being some Prose Recrea-
tions of a Rhymer. Second Edition. Cr. 8vo. 5s. net.
New York : Macmillan & Co.
THE PRINCE'S QUEST. AND OTHER POEMS. With a
Bibliographical Note added. Second Edition. Fcap.
8vo. 4s. 6d. net.
THE PURPLE EAST : a Series of Sonnets on England's
Desertion of Armenia. With a Frontispiece by G. F.
WATTS, R.A. Fcap. 8vo. Wrappers, 1s. net.
WATT (FRANCIS).
THE LAW'S LUMBER ROOM. Fcap. 8vo. 3s. 6d. net.
Chicago : A. C. McClurg & Co.
WATTS (THEODORE).
POEMS. Crown 8vo. 5s. net.   [*In preparation.*
There will also be an Edition de Luxe *of this volume printed at
the Kelmscott Press.*
WELLS (H. G.).
SELECT CONVERSATIONS WITH AN UNCLE. (*See* MAY-
FAIR SET.)
WHARTON (H. T.).
SAPPHO.   Memoir, Text, Selected Renderings, and a
Literal Translation by HENRY THORNTON WHARTON.
With three Illustrations in Photogravure, and a Cover
designed by AUBREY BEARDSLEY. Fcap. 8vo.
7s. 6d. net.
Chicago : A. C. McClurg & Co.

THE YELLOW BOOK
An Illustrated Quarterly
Pott 4to.   5s. net.
VOLUME I.   April 1894.   272 pages.   15 Illustrations.
                                          [*Out of print.*
VOLUME II.   July 1894.   364 pages.   23 Illustrations.
VOLUME III. October 1894.   280 pages.   15 Illustrations.
VOLUME IV.   January 1895.   285 pages.   16 Illustrations.
VOLUME V.   April 1895.   317 pages.   14 Illustrations.
VOLUME VI.   July 1895.   335 pages.   16 Illustrations.
VOLUME VII. October 1895.   320 pages.   20 Illustrations.
VOLUME VIII. January 1896.   406 pages.   26 Illustrations.
Boston : Copeland & Day.

www.ingramcontent.com/pod-product-compliance
Lightning Source LLC
Chambersburg PA
CBHW031104020726
47495CB00007B/2046